# THE SUMMER I FOUND HOME

PART OF THE SUMMERS IN SEASIDE SERIES

AMANDA SHELLEY

Visit my website at
www.amandashelley.com

# CONNECT WITH AMANDA SHELLEY

Want to be the first to know about upcoming sales and new releases? Make sure you sign up for my newsletter as well as connect with me on social media and your favorite retail store.

Website:
www.amandashelley.com
Newsletter:
https://geni.us/AmandaShelleyNL
Facebook:
https://www.facebook.com/authoramandashelley/
Instagram:
https://www.instagram.com/authoramandashelley/
Reader's Group:
https://www.facebook.com/groups/AmandasArmyofReaders/
Tik Tok:
https://www.tiktok.com/@authoramandashelley
Amazon:
https://www.amazon.com/author/amandashelley
Goodreads:
https://www.goodreads.com/author/show/19713563.Amanda_Shelley
Book Bub:
https://www.bookbub.com/profile/amanda-shelley

**Being a pilot is all I've ever known.**

I served my country, and I'm damn proud of my career.

But sacrifices were made, especially when it came to family.

I've missed first steps, first days of school, and first dates, to name a few.

My kids grew up. They're having families of their own.

*Was it worth it?*

When an opportunity brings me to Seaside, I jump in feet first, no questions asked.

It means experiencing all those firsts with my grandkids.

With family as my focus and my guard down, I don't even see Faye coming.

She may have been my first love, but I quickly learn she's a force to be reckoned with and has me holding on for dear life.

*I thought our ship had sailed, but now that I'm home for good, I just might get more than one second chance.*

# Chapter 1
## Mark

My eyes pop open, and without even looking at a clock, I know it's zero five hundred. I just feel it. Hell, it's been ingrained into every fiber of my being for the last thirty-plus years. Should I really be surprised?

"You're supposed to be retired," I groan in frustration. "What was the point of buying blackout curtains if I can't even sleep until oh seven hundred?"

Maybe I should ask my daughters how they sleep-trained their toddlers?

*Is it even possible to change your sleeping habits at forty-eight?*

I *could* get up and go to the diner for breakfast. But the regulars are more my mother's age than mine. Hell, last time I went in, one man told me how he'd been sweet on my mother for years.

Of course, everyone loved Jane Lancaster.

I love my mom and miss her like crazy; she was so vibrant and full of life. I'm honored when people tell me as much. I'm thankful she found Seaside to call her home, but I have no business knowing about any of her romantic interludes.

Rolling over, I finally glance at the clock that illuminates the room.

Yep, I'm right.

Zero five zero six flashes on the screen.

Knowing I'll never get back to sleep, I toss the covers aside and get up.

I hate wasting the day away, but with the sound ordinance of the city, my project can't start until zero seven hundred.

*Welp... I may as well use this time to work out.*

On autopilot, my body goes through the motions of getting ready. Before I make a conscious effort, my shoes are laced, and I'm stretched and ready to run. I've got a route I love following now that I've returned to Seaside. It takes me right past my daughters' homes—though they're rarely up at this hour unless their children decide to bless them with an early morning wakeup.

As my feet hit the pavement, and the cool misty sea fog fills my lungs, my mind drifts to the reason I've returned to this sleepy town. I could've retired literally anywhere in the world, but thanks to Mom and her love of Seaside, Oregon, my daughters have all somehow settled here.

At eighteen, I couldn't wait to leave this place. I had dreams of joining the Air Force and traveling the world. I worked my ass off in high school and had most of my undergraduate degree before graduating high school, thanks to our local community college. I couldn't wait to attend the Air Force Academy and complete my pilot training.

Then I met Sarah.

I fell hard and fast for that woman. When we got pregnant with Lanie, a mere six weeks after meeting, I married her, thinking I could have it all: a wife, a kid, and the possibility of a phenomenal career in the Air Force.

As I moved my way up in rank, my family grew. I swear, Sarah and I got pregnant by merely looking at each other. Of course, we never knew twins ran in my family until Sloane and Raven were born.

*God, that was a wild and crazy time.*

I was running on caffeine and adrenaline, trying to help as much as I could, while moving up in rank. I felt horrible being deployed after the kids came along, but Sarah insisted we'd be okay.

We were, for a few more years—or looking back, maybe we weren't.

I could tell she was tired and stressed to the max. I tried to do what I could from afar, but it's not like I could hop on a plane and come home. The Air Force owned my ass for the next six years.

I'd never felt more helpless in my life.

Mom was a saint. She visited as much as she could when I was deployed. It was a huge relief knowing Sarah wasn't alone with three children under the age of three.

When I returned home, Mom thought she was doing us a favor by insisting we spend some time together—that's how Lizzy arrived nine months later. I swear, we were careful, but apparently, we were destined for baby number four in four years.

For a while after Lizzy was born, I thought things were back on track. We were making it work. While I was deployed to Afghanistan that next year, everything changed. Sarah decided she couldn't do *us* any longer, and I essentially got the worst letter of my life.

God, it sounds fucking ridiculous all these years later, admitting I got a *Dear John* letter, but that's what it was. I loved her enough to let her go—plain and simple. I knew I couldn't be the husband she needed, and ultimately, she deserved better than me.

Since that day, I vowed to be the best father I could, even from afar. When stationed around the world, I moved heaven and earth to spend time with my girls. I insisted their lives remain as normal as possible, but I wanted them with me as much as they could be on breaks from school and during each summer. Mom was crucial in helping me keep our parenting plan in place throughout the years. I don't know what I would've done without her.

I've met a few women over the years, but since time was a limited resource, and I spent every spare moment with my daughters, nothing ever worked out. My girls will always come first. It's as simple as that.

When my wrist vibrates with an incoming text, I stop to read it.

HARPER:

Have a quick in-and-out that shouldn't take more than a day or two. You interested?

Enzo Harper is a good buddy of mine from flight school. Since his retirement about ten years ago, he's worked for a private security firm based in Portland. They not only protect civilians, but they also do contract work for the government. I've been on a few joint missions and know Riggs runs a tight operation.

After retiring, they were down a pilot and called in a favor. It was a quick transport flight from Portland to LA. Not only did it get me back in the air, but it gave me an opportunity to do what I've spent my life training for.

It was the best of both worlds: I got into the action but wasn't committed to anything beyond that mission. Best of all, I made it home just in time for Milli's school performance without my family being any the wiser.

ME:

What time is wheels up?

Harper's response is immediate.

HARPER:

Depends on how fast you can get here. Riggs has the plane on standby at SIA when you're ready.

Shit, there goes my plans for the day. Guess my project will have to wait. They must need me if they've already got the plane ready at the airfield in Seaside.

Riggs insisted on having one housed here if they needed me. I just didn't expect it to be so soon.

ME:

Finishing a run—wheels up in 90.

HARPER:

Roger That. See you soon.

Without another thought, I flip over to the family group chat.

I swear now that I'm retired, my girls are worse than my mother ever was about my whereabouts. They don't want or expect details, but they have asked I keep them apprised when I leave town.

ME:

Helping Riggs again. Be home in a few days. Can someone come get the food I have set out for family dinner tomorrow night if I'm not back? There's enough to feed an entire squadron. Don't let it go to waste.

My youngest is surprisingly the first to reply.

LIZZY:

Sure thing. We'll host at my house either way. I'll swing by and pick everything up while Milli's at a friend's house this afternoon.

Before I can respond, another text comes through.

LIZZY:

Love you. Safe Travels.

ME:

Roger that. Love you all.

Suddenly, my schedule is cleared.

Just as I return home and slow to a walk, I notice a woman in a baggy cardigan and leggings bringing out the trash to the end of the driveway next door. She's struggling with the can as it gets stuck in a rut.

I almost offer to help, but the can crests the hole just as I approach.

"This can will be the death of me," she grumbles and shakes her head.

Unable to help myself, I joke, "I think it's the driveway's fault, not the can's. Clearly, the pothole is the culprit."

When she looks up, her jaw drops, and her eyes blink rapidly.

"Mark Lancaster... is... that you?"

Recognition hits hard, and my heart races as if I've just sprinted a marathon. Electricity zips through my spine as she scrutinizes my features.

Faye Ames, my high school sweetheart, stands before me, and I feel like a fish out of water, floundering for what to say.

"Yeah... it's me," I whisper in disbelief. I've always wondered what happened to her. We were thick as thieves for the longest time, but after graduation, we parted ways, and I haven't heard from her since. "What are you doing here?"

A perfectly sculpted brow arches as she smirks. "I should ask you the same thing. I thought you were off saving the world... at least, that's what Mom says."

Well, *that* piques my interest.

"You've been asking about me?"

Sighing heavily, she grins as she shakes her head. "Not you specifically, but my mom, as well as yours, filled me in on a few things over the years when I've visited." She winces, then quickly adds, "I'm so sorry to hear about your mom, by the way."

Even though it's been a few years, "Thank you" comes out as a rote response whenever someone mentions her.

Rubbing a hand down my face, I admit, "Mom never mentioned anything about keeping up with you."

"Probably because I asked her not to. Jane was one of my favorite people. When I stopped in to visit Mom, Jane and I always took the time to catch up."

A lot is packed into that ramble, but one thing hits clear.

"You... Asked her not to?"

Shrugging guiltily, she sighs. "It seems stupid now, but you leaving for the Air Force hit hard... So, I left early for college... Then you got married... And it was just best to leave things alone. Eventually, too much time had passed, and I didn't think it would matter."

Before I can think better of it, I quickly add, "Did Mom mention during any of that time... I also got divorced?" The words fly out of my mouth.

*Holy shit, I can't believe she's really here.*

My mind reels as my past crashes into the present.

At one point, Faye was my best friend—my ride or die. We were tight from the moment we met. Then our connection turned into more, junior year. When I set my sights on the Air Force, she fully supported that decision and was a huge factor in getting me to push hard to reach my dreams.

Near the end of our senior year, we called things off. She'd had an early acceptance to NYU, and I was off to boot camp once I turned eighteen at the end of summer. We knew the odds of a relationship surviving distance were low, so we parted ways and eventually lost touch.

I've often wondered what happened to her, but obviously, I never reached out, so that's on me.

Faye's smile is as beautiful as ever when she shrugs sheepishly and pushes a loose strand of hair behind her ear that has fallen from the top knot she has her hair piled in. "Yeah... But you had your hands full with four amazing girls. I never wanted to get in the way."

"You know about my girls?"

Rolling her eyes, her infamous smirk forms.

"Of course. They were all Jane could talk about. She was so proud of them. Besides, her house was plastered with photos. I could see for myself what an amazing family you had."

"Just how often did you visit?"

"Not as often as I should've, obviously. But enough, over the years. I was in London when your mom passed, or I would have been at the service. She was a special woman."

My head spins with so many questions, but one works its

way out of my mouth before I can think better of it. "Why didn't you ever reach out?"

She darts her eyes to the ground as her teeth bite into her lower lip for a few heartbeats before squaring her shoulders and meeting my gaze. "What can I say...? I was young and protecting my heart."

*Protecting her heart—from what?*

For the first time in forever, guilt crashes in. Our falling out of touch is just as much on me. But something doesn't settle right. "Was I that unapproachable?"

Again, on a long sigh, she shakes her head. "No. It was harder than I thought to be on my own across the country. I didn't really want any reminders of home. But then, too much time had passed, and you'd clearly moved on, so I kept my distance."

Her truth makes my chest feel tight and my skin itch.

Not knowing what to say, I glance at the house behind her. "Did your parents move?"

"No, they're still in the same place." Thumbing over her shoulder, she adds, "I'm renting this place because, as much as I love my parents, living with them permanently isn't an option."

She's been living beside me this entire time, and I had no idea?

*Some special operator I am—don't even notice who my neighbors are?*

How could I miss this?

"I could've sworn when I moved in, your place was vacant."

On a breezy laugh, she shrugs again. "I've been out of town on business for the last six weeks."

Well, that makes sense.

`My wrist buzzes, and I'm brought back to reality.

My ass needs to get to the airfield, pronto.

Running a hand through my hair, I lay my truth on the line,

"Look, Faye, I'm heading out of town myself for a few days and need to leave ASAP. Please don't take this as a brush-off. Can I get your number and call you when I return?"

Her gorgeous blue eyes bore into mine. They're brighter in this morning light. Just when I'm certain she's going to brush me off, a coy smile plays at her lips, and she spews out her digits. Then adds, "I sure hope your memory hasn't faded in all these years." A triumphant smile fills her features as she winks for good measure.

"Glad to see you're as sassy as ever," I smirk, falling into old habits. "Be expecting a call when I return."

Rolling her eyes in the most adorable way, she laughs, "Always so bossy."

She turns and starts walking away, but I call after her. "Faye?"

Pausing mid-stride, she glances back.

Once her eyes meet mine, I vow, "I'm older now, and I won't be making the same mistake twice."

"What's that?" she asks, curiosity filling her features.

"I'm not letting you ghost me again."

# Chapter 2
## Faye

From the moment I saw Mark yesterday morning, I haven't stopped thinking about him. How the hell did he become my neighbor?

What are the odds of us both being back here?

As I sip my morning coffee and try to get a handle on the day, I can't help but recall the endless conversations from our past. He was adamant about leaving this small town and seeing the world. I can't imagine him considering this place home once again.

*Wait—If he's here full time, why isn't he living at his mom's house?*

That place is gorgeous and has the best views of the ocean.

I know some work was done on it a few years back.

Did they sell it? What does it mean that he's returned, and why is he living next door?

Why the hell is thinking about him making my heart race like I'm back in high school? It's been thirty years, for fuck's sake. He shouldn't have this type of impact on me. I'm a grown-ass woman, and we literally spoke for less than five minutes.

*Sheesh, get it together, Faye.*

I swear it was as if no time had passed when my eyes met his.

Tingles sprinted down my spine, and my heart fluttered uncontrollably.

Mark is the only man on earth who's had that effect on me.

*He's also the only one I ever let make an impact like that.*

Hell, I was with Corey for nearly a decade, and when things ended, I was happier to be rid of him than to mourn the loss of what we had.

Though that likely had more to do with the fact that he had been cheating on me.

*Yeah, that's certainly the case.*

After I learned Mark got married, I put all my focus on finishing my degree and building my career. Then I was recruited as a cybersecurity analyst for a prominent firm that had me traveling across Europe frequently.

I didn't have time to mourn the loss of our friendship or the life we could've had together, had I not insisted we break up. I met Corey right after grad school. He was just as ambitious as I was to further himself in his career, so it worked—until it didn't.

Looking back, our relationship was more of convenience than of true love.

*Maybe that's why it never worked out?*

As much as I'd wanted kids when I was younger, it was never the right time.

*Or maybe I just never found the right person?*

By the time I finished school, I spent my thirties with the wrong man, chasing my career. Then in my forties, I found myself again.

Don't get me wrong, I love the life I live.

I have amazing friends and family and have traveled the world at a whim.

Now, instead of working for a corporate conglomerate, I'm an independent contractor. As long as there is internet, I can essentially work from anywhere in the world, and nothing ties me down.

That is, until my dad had his health scare last year.

I immediately returned to Seaside and have been here ever since. Sure, I still travel now and then, but this small town has once again become my home base.

With my siblings having families of their own, the flexibility of my schedule allows me to be there for my parents when they need it most. Between doctor appointments, physical therapy, cooking meals, and being here for emotional support, who knew parenting your parents could be more difficult than climbing a corporate career?

Thankfully, Dad has bounced back and is making a full recovery.

As I look out my window to the house next door, Mark's parting words slice through my heart for the millionth time.

*"I'm not letting you ghost me again."*

His tone was jovial, and the twinkle in his eye was his tell for an attempt to be lighthearted—some things never change. However, his directness hit just as hard. Mark's never been one to mince words, and despite ghosting not even being a thing when it happened, it is, in fact, what I did.

As my eyes roam the two-story craftsman-style house next door, I can tell that in the time I've been away, Mark has made some upgrades. Not only is there a fresh coat of paint, but it looks as if he's replaced all the windows and created an enclosed porch with a custom gate.

Does he have pets?

Is he still in the Air Force?

Maybe he's finally retired.

*What does it mean that he's returned to Seaside?*

I still can't believe Mark, of all people, moved in next door without me knowing.

Millions of questions fly through my mind as I stare at the house next door. He's made that charming rental house into a home. Does this mean he's in Seaside for good?

A loud knock at my door jolts me out of my reverie and makes my heart race.

It's seven in the morning; who would be here at this time of day?

*Uh... You saw Mark much earlier than this yesterday,* I chastely remind myself as I run a hand through my hair and bolt toward the door.

Breathless, I rush to the entry. Pausing for the briefest of moments, I compose myself before eagerly swinging the door open.

Only to be met by no one.

*What the hell?*

That's when I hear the distinct sound of a delivery truck door rolling before slamming shut from the street, and my heart sinks.

Looking at my feet, I finally see the package laying on the porch.

Chuckling to myself, I bend to retrieve it, then look around to see if anyone witnessed me acting the fool.

Thank God, I get to keep this incident to myself.

"That's what you get for being so worked up over that man," I muse at myself before returning to my morning coffee.

My body vibrates from that short burst of adrenaline, and it's obvious coffee is the last thing I need. Just the thought of Mark is enough to make me wired. If I finish this cup, I'll be jumping at every sound I hear.

Taking my mug to the kitchen, I dump the rest in the sink, rinse it out, and put it in the dishwasher.

Knowing I'll never survive the day sitting around, waiting on a call from Mark, I make a split decision and reach for my phone and dial the number I've had memorized my entire life.

Three rings later, I rush out, "Want to meet up for breakfast?" before they can even say hello.

A deep chuckle comes through the phone. "Good morning to you, too, sweet girl."

"Sorry, Dad. Too much coffee... Obviously. But you're the only one I know who's up this early. Want to meet me at the diner?"

"Hmmm... Your mom's still sleeping..." Dad pretends to mull over my proposition.

"Got a better offer?" I tease, knowing he's got nothing planned today. He's been told to take it easy and has been going stir-crazy for quite some time.

"I suppose we could meet up... *if* you keep your mouth quiet about my hankering for bacon."

"Deal. See you in twenty?" I quickly agree.

"Ha. What's the rush, Faye?"

"Can't a girl be hungry?" I counter, not wanting to get into it with him. Besides, there's not much to say. What would I tell him? *I ran into Mark. We spoke for what... five minutes? Oh, and Dad, Mark's got me so worked up, I'm jumping at every sound in my house, I can't concentrate for shit, and I need to get the hell out of Dodge just to stop thinking about him.*

Yeah, I'm not going there with Dad. He always liked Mark, but as far as he's concerned, that ship sailed years ago.

*But a morning with Dad could distract me.*

"While we're out, want to run some errands with me?"

"What type of errands?" he counters hesitantly. "I'm not up for aimlessly traipsing from shop to shop, like you and your mother enjoy."

"I won't torture you like that," I promise. "But I know you

never miss going to the hardware store. I need a bracket for that shelf in the bathroom, and Mom asked me to pick up some things for her at the grocery store."

"Okay, kiddo," Dad muses. "You've twisted my arm. I'll see you in twenty."

Before I can say another word, he disconnects the call.

Shaking my head, I rush to my room with one hope in mind: *Will this distraction be enough to keep me from thinking about the man next door?*

# Chapter 3
## Mark

Three days.

It's been three days since bumping into Faye.

Three days of itching to reach out, knowing I couldn't afford the distraction.

Mission first, always.

Lives were at stake, and thankfully, I've mastered the art of compartmentalization.

The extraction was gnarly and put my skills to the test. Riggs was right to request my assistance, and I'm glad I could help. Being back on his team gives me a sense of purpose, even if I'm no longer the one calling the shots. I not only exfilled our team safely but also made good time getting us back to PDX once the mission was complete.

I'm still flying high from our team's success as I touch down in Seaside. I routinely go through my post-flight checks, and the next thing I know, I'm heading down the highway toward home.

I've always prided myself on being direct, but as I close the distance between Faye and me, I fear I'm heading into uncharted territory. I haven't truly spoken to her since we were kids. Now that we're neighbors, she'll know the second I arrive home. I need a game plan, or I'll be up shit's creek without a paddle before I even have the chance to hop out of my truck.

She was always quick to see right through me.

She's likely the only woman who ever has.

The way her eyes heated as she rattled off her digits as a challenge made my heart race and my mind work overtime. My visceral response was unexpected.

*How can just one little smile take me back thirty years?*

More importantly, did I have the same effect on her?

Hell, I've already been zero contact for three fucking days.

She probably thinks I'm an asshole and not interested in reconnecting.

Which couldn't be farther from the truth.

I haven't stopped thinking about her since forcing myself to leave.

I'm dying to know what she's been up to. Is she married, does she have any kids, and most pressingly, what's made her return to Seaside?

My fingers have hovered over her number more times than I can count since programming it into my phone. The only thing that's stopped me is this hard truth—our first real chance at catching up shouldn't be an awkward phone call.

Faye deserves better than that.

Stopping at one of the few lights in town, I contemplate parking and just pulling the trigger to get this much-needed call over with.

Just as my thumb hovers over the call button, doubt creeps in.

*What the fuck should I even say?*

I've been radio silent since seeing her.

She probably thinks I'm blowing her off, and my leaving

town is merely a throwaway excuse to get away from her, which obviously isn't true. But how do I tell her that?

Hell, I can't stop thinking about her.

She's got me feeling like a sixteen-year-old again, twisting me from the inside out. I'm dying to know what she's been up to. We used to be connected at the hip.

I know for me, life happened.

When she stopped reaching out, I moved on.

Then I met Sarah, and she and the girls consumed every second of my time. Is that the case for Faye?

Does she have a family of her own?

I didn't see a ring on her finger.

Maybe she's single like me?

That thought alone excites me more than it should.

I've never reacted to a woman the way I do Faye.

*But is this just my memory playing tricks on me?*

It has been a while since I've attempted to date anyone.

*Maybe I'm just out of practice?*

*So, call her, dumbass.*

It's the only way I'll finally know which end is up.

My fingers hover over her number, and I hesitate once again.

The light changes, and I start driving.

Each second I get closer to home, I'm closer to Faye. I know without a doubt, I want to see her tonight, but the question remains—is she up for seeing me?

*For fuck's sake, Lancaster. Get it together.*

I've commanded thousands of airmen and have made life and death decisions without a second glance. I can certainly call *this* woman.

At one point, she was my best fucking friend.

*Man up and fucking do it already.*

When my stomach growls, I make a split-second decision

and pull off to the side of the road. Instead of calling, I quickly tap out a text:

ME:

I'll be home in twenty. Have you eaten dinner?

There. I've made contact.

All I can do now is wait and see if she responds.

# Chapter 4
## Faye

When my phone buzzes with an incoming text, I stare at it for the longest time.



I knew it was Mark before I even stopped reading.

Of course, in typical Mark fashion, he's completely thrown me off guard.

What the hell do I even make of this?

Who sends shit like this to someone they haven't spoken to in thirty years?

I know our interaction was awkward at best the other morning, but it's rather presumptuous that I'd be available for dinner.

*Be home in twenty*—Does that mean he expects me to join him?

Who does that?

After three days of no contact, the thought of seeing him again makes my stomach feel as if bulls are stampeding, rather than butterflies swarming inside me. My connection to Mark has always been intense. But this is beyond ridiculous.

I'm not some young schoolgirl talking to her first crush. I'm a grown woman, for crying out loud.

Reading through the text for what feels like the millionth time, I'm still flabbergasted.

Wait—was this even meant for me?

Surely, this type of text is meant for someone he's familiar with. Maybe he's got family in town or—crap, he's seeing someone and texted me by accident?

As I stare at my phone, willing his words to make sense, another text comes through.

UNKNOWN NUMBER:

> Either you're busy or overanalyzing who sent you this.

A laugh rips through my body, and the tension I'd been feeling releases instantly.

Before I can respond, another text comes through.

UNKNOWN NUMBER:

> I should have started with, "This is Mark." I just got home, and if you're free, I'd love to have you join me for dinner. Are French dip sandwiches still your favorite? Pop's has the best prime rib in town. Now that we're of age, we can legally share a beer—or hard cider in your case.

UNKNOWN NUMBER:

> I'm standing outside your door. Should I knock or head out solo?

Sure enough, there's a dark shadow hovering behind the stained-glass window at the top of the door. If I thought he was direct before, but this takes things to an entirely new level.

Mark certainly doesn't mince words or waste time.

My body flushes with heat, and my gut swirls like I'm about to be hit by a category 5 hurricane. Gulping hard, I dart my eyes to the door in question, but my body's frozen in place.

When three loud raps on the door echo through the room, my body jumps into action, and my legs finally remember their primary function.

Swinging open the door, a smile plays at my lips as I take in his large form.

Damn, he's as gorgeous as ever.

His hair is a little longer than it was when he entered the Air Force, but it's still got that high and tight feel to it. What was once jet black now has a light sprinkling of gray around the temples. His face is still square and angular, but with a few more laugh lines, and those perceptive hazel eyes drink me in entirely.

Our years apart have been kind to him.

My mouth dries as I take in his black fitted tee that shows off his broad shoulders, sculpted arms, and muscular chest.

Damn. Time has been more than good to him.

*How is it possible he's even more handsome now?*

The distinct sound of his throat clearing effectively draws me out of my perusal. With a quirk of his brow and a playful smirk set on his face, he asks, "If you're done taking inventory, can I do something I should have done the moment I saw you the other day?"

*And what's that?*

Without a word, he steps forward and envelops me in one of the tightest hugs I've had in recent memory. Instead of feeling awkward, Mark's strong arms ground me. I revel in his masculine scent. Inhaling deeply, my body relaxes, and the stress of the past three days melts away. He smells of sandalwood, fresh air, and something that is always uniquely him.

The strong beat of his heart reminds me of how I used to claim this spot on his chest as mine. A smile tugs at my lips with the memory.

*Oh, to be that young and carefree again.*

Mark always was one of the best huggers I know, and I'm glad to see some things never change.

"What are you smiling at, Faye? Do I smell or something?"

A laugh escapes before I can think better of it. Patting him on the chest, I shake my head. "No, you smell just fine. Wait... How could you tell I was smiling?"

Pulling back to look him in the eye, my stomach dips when his sexy smirk forms, and his head shakes slightly.

"It's one of your tells. Your fist clenches, and you nuzzle in further."

"My tells? Since when do I have tells?"

"Since always," he says on a sigh.

Rolling my eyes, I grin at his audacity. "You think you know me so well, Mark Lancaster. A lot of time has passed. You might be wrong, ya know."

Scratching the side of his nose, he raises a brow. "Were you not smiling just now?"

Shit. He's got me there. "Maybe."

"So..." he draws out, "what were you thinking about, then?"

There's no way I'm telling him how good he smells. If my memory serves me correctly, his ego won't fit in the room if I do.

When I don't say anything, his head cocks to the side and asks, "So, about that dinner... You interested?"

"What makes you so sure I'm free? I could have plans."

Heat fills his hazel eyes, and my belly lights on fire with his sudden intense stare.

"You wouldn't have been looking at me like that if you had someone special in your life."

Well, shit, he's got me there.

After thirty years, how can this man still have this effect on me?

# Chapter 5
## Mark

The breath Faye holds as she stares into my eyes nearly guts me.

It's like she's taken all the air from the room, and I can no longer breathe.

But I just hold her gaze and wait for confirmation.

I'm hardly wrong when it comes to reading people—Hell, I'm not even sure why I said it, but the words were out before I could think better of it.

I've spent every spare moment of the last three days thinking about this woman, and I need to know if it's all in my head, or if she's feeling whatever this is, too.

"I... Uh..." She fidgets, then looks anywhere but at me.

When she shifts her weight back and forth from foot to foot, guilt crashes in. Beating around the bush costs lives, and I've gotten in the habit of never mincing words.

That may be a great tactic while on missions, but as I watch her cheeks darken, I'm thinking I might've been a bit too direct.

However, it feels as if a lot is riding on her answer, and

honestly, for some reason beyond me, I need to know where she stands.

Hesitantly, I step forward and let her off the hook. "Look, Faye, if there is someone special in your life, I'd never get in the way."

Squaring her shoulders, she finally meets my gaze. "No... I don't suppose you would."

Now, it's my turn to be caught off guard.

"What does that mean?"

Reaching out, she takes my hand and squeezes it gently. "That's just not who you are."

Damn straight. There's no way in hell I'd step in on someone else's girl. Even if she's the only one I've been able to think about since seeing her again.

I may not like it, but I'd never interfere.

"So... does that mean you *do* have someone special?"

Faye gasps, and her eyes widen like saucers. "Oh, hell... I'm really messing this up." Shaking her head profusely, she quickly adds, "No... There's no one else."

Relief floods through me, and I jerk her into another hug. "Good, because it's been way too long since we've caught up."

With her body pressed firmly against mine, I find myself finally relaxing into her.

I swear we're so close, she feels my stomach rumble before it makes a sound, and a beautiful giggle fills the room. "You really do need food, don't you? Let's go before you famish in my foyer. Pop's is one of my favorites."

Running a hand down my face, I admit, "Yeah, it's been a minute since I've eaten." I was so hell-bent on getting back to Seaside, it never crossed my mind. But the way her smile lights up her face in amusement makes my hurry worth it, even if it is at my expense.

"Just give me a sec to grab everything, and we can go," she says, stepping away.

As she gathers her things, I take this opportunity to fully take her in. She has this air of sophistication, yet she remains casual for this beach town. She's wearing an ice-blue tank that accentuates her toned arms and makes her eyes brighter than I remember. Memories of how those beautiful blues could get me to do just about anything with a simple glance vividly return with a vengeance.

As she tucks a loose strand of hair behind her ear, I take note of the subtle highlights streaking through her dark-blonde hair when light hits it just right. When we were younger, she'd always wear it in a long braid to keep the beach wind from having its way with it, but now, it's cut in long, wavy layers just below her shoulders. I can't help but wonder if she still enjoys riding with the windows down and letting it blow all around her.

As she bends over to grab a pair of sandals by the door, my eyes are drawn to the way her dark-gray, cargo-style joggers hug her sexy curves and fit like they were made for her.

Time has certainly been good to Faye.

She effortlessly looks comfortable, yet sophisticated. My daughters call it casual chic—if I remember correctly. She's got this timeless look about her.

Grabbing her purse from the side table and a denim jacket from the coat tree beside it, she turns to me with a smile. "I'm ready if you are."

Opening the door behind me, I lead her outside.

The moment she spots my truck in her driveway, I catch the slight shake of her head as a smile forms on her lips. Her head turns just as I'm certain her eyes roll, but I can't be sure.

"Something wrong?" I ask, reaching to open her door.

Faye simply shakes her head and climbs into the cab of my

truck as if she's been doing it for years. "Nope. Just get in and drive, Lancaster." As I shut her door, I swear I hear, "Yeesh... Some things never change."

Chuckling, I do as I'm told.

Once I've backed out of her driveway, heading toward Pop's, I ask, "Have you been living in Seaside long?"

"Just over a year."

If she's been living here a year, how the hell did I not notice her next door when I moved in? "What type of business are you in, if you're leaving town for nearly six weeks at a time?"

"I'm a cybersecurity consultant. My client in London was onboarding a new branch of their business. I was tasked to set up their network and ensure there weren't any data breaches as they expanded."

She always was brilliant, but I can't say I was expecting this. "Do you work in the private sector or with government agencies?"

I catch a slight shrug as she confirms my suspicion. "Both. This time, it was for a private company. But I do have government contracts with the DOD from time to time."

"Interesting..." I draw out, allowing me time to mull over my next question. Department of Defense contracts are hard to come by. She must be top-notch to land those. However, in true Faye fashion, she interjects before I can continue.

Her spine straightens as her head turns my way. "Just what is that supposed to mean?"

Exhaling heavier than I should, I admit, "I find your line of work interesting... Nothing more than that. I've always wondered where you ended up. In high school, you were one of the smartest people I knew. It's good to see you put that big brain of yours to work. Have you always been an independent contractor?"

"Only for the last ten years. Before that, I worked out of

New York with a company that handled cybersecurity for major corporations as well as the DOD. It's how I've kept my foot in the door as an independent contractor."

"How did I not know this?" I muse aloud, more to myself than expecting an answer.

I feel like a total ass for not reaching out to her at some point.

All defensiveness disappears as she reaches for my arm and gives it a gentle squeeze. "Our paths never crossed, Mark. How *would* you know?"

"I suppose you're right," I concede as I pull into a street parking spot in front of Pop's Hops.

"I usually am." She grins widely and rolls her eyes, then reaches for the door handle. "We've got plenty of time for catching up, Lancaster. No need to worry about it all happening at once. You're starving. Let's go eat."

With that, she hops out of my truck, and I'm left gaping like an idiot.

She always could call me on my shit like no other.

*Glad to see some things haven't changed.*

By the time she takes a few steps, my brain kicks in, and my body goes double time to catch up with her. My long strides eat up the distance between us, and just before she makes it to the door, I reach out to open it and hold it open for her.

"Thanks," is whispered as she walks in and waits by the sign to be seated.

I barely step up beside her when a waiter greets us. "Welcome. Would you like a table inside, under the patio, or near the bar?"

Faye glances my way, and I nod, suggesting she make our choice, as I have no preference.

"The patio is fine."

On the way to our table, we learn about tonight's specials,

as well as some of the newest brews they've acquired. He also informs us that a live band will start soon and advises us to sit adjacent to one another if we want a better view of the stage.

Sitting next to Faye is no hardship, that's for sure.

I pull out the chair with the most direct view of the stage and motion for her to take a seat. The scent of vanilla, lavender, and something uniquely her washes over me, and memories from our summers here in Seaside surface.

As soon as we're both seated, the waiter slides a menu toward Faye, but she shakes him off. "Oh, I don't need one, I already know what I want, and this guy"—she points at me with a wicked gleam—"promised me a French dip. Can I get a pint of Puckering Pear, as well?"

"What's a puckering pear?" spews out of my mouth before either of them says more.

Rolling those beautiful blues my way, she smirks indignantly. "Only one of the best microbrews."

"It's distributed from Bedknobs and Brews in Colorado," the waiter eagerly adds. "It's popular this time of year."

Always down for something new, I shrug. "I'll take a pint of that, as well as a French dip."

"Excellent choice. I'll put your order in and get it out to you as soon as I can."

The moment he walks away, she turns to me and sighs heavily. "Of all the gin joints in all the world, how did you... Mark Lancaster, become my neighbor?"

"I should ask you the same thing." I laugh.

*Casablanca* was always one of her favorite movies. She was a fan of the classics. I can't imagine that ever changing.

"Seriously, Lancaster... How did you end up in Seaside? You were hell-bent on leaving town. I can't for the life of me fathom you settling here."

"It's not that unfathomable," I deadpan and hold her gaze.

A perfectly sculpted brow arches my way. "Are you always this evasive?"

*Only when I know it gets you riled up.*

When she doesn't back down from the staring contest I've perpetuated, I eventually give in with a shrug. "It's simple. My kids."

Her brows knit together as she studies me further. "What do you mean?"

"Where they go, I go. Now that I'm retired, and Uncle Sam isn't dictating where I live, I'm determined to spend as much time with my girls and their growing families as possible."

From the way her eyes widen, she obviously didn't expect this response.

"Families? More than one of your kids lives here?"

A low laugh escapes as I think about my daughters and the chaos their families bring. "All four of them, along with their husbands and gaggle of kids."

"Wow..." Faye whispers. "The last time I visited your mom, she told me a story about teaching your youngest to drive." Her eyes go wide as saucers as she says, "Are you telling me she's already married?"

I can't help the low laugh that escapes. Faye's shocked expression is adorable.

"Yep." I nod proudly. "Lizzy's not only married but has three kids."

My revelation makes her jaw drop in disbelief. "You're. A. Grandpa?" The words come out as if each one is its own sentence, and it takes everything in me not to laugh at the dumbfounded expression on her beautiful face.

Shrugging, I admit, "They call me Papa, but same difference."

"Wow... I didn't see that coming." She's quiet for a moment, then adds, "You already have three grandkids?"

"Actually..." I puff out my chest in pride. "I've got nine."

"Holy shit... I really stepped in it this time," Faye mutters just barely loud enough to hear.

Her eyes look anywhere but at me, then they close for the briefest of seconds before she takes a deep breath and adds, "I am so sorry for presuming anything. I never had any kids, and I don't feel old... But..." she pauses and exaggeratedly looks me over, then quickly adds, "you *really* don't look like a grandpa. Hell, you're not even fifty."

Amusement washes over me as I watch her attempt to dig herself out of a hole.

To save her from herself, I quickly point out, "I started early... Remember. Add in four daughters and the fact that twins run in our family, and they multiply quickly."

Nodding slowly, she sighs heavily. "I can imagine.... And they all live here?"

"Yep." I smile with delight. "Two of them even married locals."

And apparently, I'm just full of surprises for Faye.

"You're kidding me. What are the odds of your daughters settling in the one town you couldn't wait to leave?"

"Mom had everything to do with it, I'm certain." I chuckle at the memory. "Before she passed, she made arrangements for her home to be renovated without bothering to enlighten anyone of said plans."

"Your mom *would* do something like that," Faye muses. "She always was a planner."

"You can say that again." I chuckle at the memory. "Lanie, my oldest, got quite a surprise when the poor, unsuspecting contractor showed up. He was just doing the job he'd been paid for, but he scared the hell out of her... And in true Lancaster fashion, she went ten toes down with him without a second thought, even though she's nearly a foot shorter than him."

She's still indignant about the situation, but to hear her husband tell it, it had to have been quite the sight.

"Between you and Jane, I'm certain your girls can stand on their own. She never let anyone get away with anything."

"No, she didn't," I agree on a sigh. "But we got Ryan out of her meddling, so I'm grateful for it."

"Ryan... Wait... are you talking about Jack Murdock's son?"

"Yeah, why?" How would she know that?

"He and his dad are the ones who helped install the ramp at my parents' house when Dad was forced to use a walker after his heart attack last year. Jack and Dad have coffee together most mornings, so when he'd heard Dad was coming home, he had the entire ramp installed within hours of getting the call. I'd never been more grateful. It was a Sunday, and they insisted on only being paid for materials. It was such a blessing to be able to get Dad safely into the house."

"How's your dad doing now?" I ask hesitantly.

"He's doing fantastic. He's back to walking three miles every day, tinkering around the house, and driving Mom nuts with his never-ending ambitions."

I can't help the chortle that escapes. "That sounds like Herb. He never was one to sit and watch paint dry."

A beautiful smile lights up her face. "Nope. Mom and I are always after him for doing too much."

"I'll probably be accused of the same things by my daughters when I'm that age. We only get so many hours in a day, ya gotta make 'em count."

Shaking her head, she gasps, "Oh, God, you're still like that?"

"Uh... You've met my mom. I'm certain that thirty years in the Air Force has only perpetuated it. How else do you think I moved up through the ranks as quickly as I did?"

Reaching out, she touches my hand. "Ambition is a good

thing, Mark. I just thought now that you've *retired,* things might have calmed down a bit."

Locking eyes with hers, I deadpan, "I may be drawing benefits from the government, but I'm far from hanging up my hat, Faye. Have you not seen the improvements I've made on the house next door?"

"The place does look good," she admits. "Though I'm surprised you're not living at your mom's."

"Mom always insisted I keep it for the girls." I shrug, then point out the obvious. "It's special to them. It's truly the only place they've ever called home for any length of time, and I'd never take those memories from them. Besides, that place is way too big for just me."

"So..." Faye draws out as if she's piecing things together, "all of your girls live there now?"

"They did... Until each of them got married. Now, it's just Lanie and her family."

Before Faye can make more presumptions, I quickly add, "Sloane bought the house next door, and Raven's got a place just down the street. Lizzy lives within walking distance—though most everything in this town is technically walking distance, I suppose."

Faye lets out a low whistle. "Wow, your girls must be doing well for themselves to nab prime real estate like that. Jane always said they were a tight bunch. I'm glad to hear things haven't changed. Though I can't imagine living that close to my siblings," she muses.

Before I can respond, she gasps, drawing my attention. "Wait... If they all live next to one another, how did *we* end up as neighbors?"

Shrugging, I add, "I looked for a place closer to them, but when the house next to yours came on the market, it was the perfect fit. It's still relatively close to everyone, and it was in decent shape but needed enough upgrades that it gave me a project to work on now that I'm *retired*." That word still tastes weird on my tongue. Sure, I still work for Riggs on occasion, but I'm retired as far as the world is concerned.

Faye's eyes narrow, and her head cocks to the side, "Retired..." Drags from her lips. "Have you actually retired, though?"

Shit. She always did see the bigger picture in things. And she's worked with the DOD. Surely, she has some idea about retired military and private security firms. "I'm no longer on Uncle Sam's payroll. I've already told you that," I pointedly remind her.

Her perfectly sculpted brow remains high. "If that's the story you're stickin' to, I'll let you have it, but if I was a betting woman..."

The waiter chooses this moment to appear with our food. After setting our plates down, he asks, "Can you think of anything else you need?"

Faye glances at me, then shakes her head.

"We're good, thanks," I assure him.

My stomach chooses this opportunity to remind me how ravenous I am, and Faye's face lights up in amusement.

Picking up her fork, she points it at me with a conspiratorial grin. "Eat, Lancaster. We've got plenty of time to catch up when you're full. Besides, I've been much too on edge these past few days to eat.... And I want to be firing on all cylinders if I'm going to decipher the double talk you're giving me."

Damn, she's good.

I fight like hell to keep the smile tugging at my lips at bay.

With a curt nod, "Roger that," slips out before I can think better of it.

# Chapter 6
## Faye

As much as I'm dying to know everything Mark's been up to, the live band jumps up on stage and starts playing. It's a group I've never heard of, but they're pretty good. They've got an alternative rock feel, though they're playing current cover songs that could be considered pop, as well.

The moment I hear the melodic opening chords of The Red Hot Chili Peppers' song "Under the Bridge," I gasp and reach for Mark's forearm to get his attention. "Ohmigosh! Do you remember that road trip we took to Seattle to see the Peppers in concert?"

He raises a brow, and a slow, sexy smile spreads across his lips. "Of course, I remember." Leaning toward me, he runs a palm along his stubbled jaw and gives a knowing smirk. "The concert was great, but I remember that trip for another reason."

Of course, he does.

It was the first time we stayed together in a hotel room, unbeknownst to our parents. Technically, our friends did go to the concert with us, but they also stayed with Jimmy Sullivan's aunt afterwards, while we went our own way.

Feigning innocence, I ask, "Would I have anything to do with that?"

This earns me an eye roll. "You know damn well you had *everything* to do with what I'm referring to." Shaking his head, he smiles. "I still can't believe Mom bought that story. It was flimsy as hell and questionable at best."

"We were such goodie two-shoes back then. We rarely did anything worth getting into trouble for."

"That our parents know of," he pointedly reminds me, and I'm surprised that, after all these years, heat flows through me at the memories.

My parents would've killed us both, should they have ever learned about everything we did that night. Nothing about us that night resembled being the goodie two-shoes everyone thought us to be.

"No shit. What our parents don't know will never hurt them."

His deep guffaw makes my spine tingle, much like it did when we were young teens in love.

Mark wasn't only my first love but my best friend. We had this instant connection that made me trust him implicitly. I'm not even sure how to describe it—what we had just existed. I've never felt anything like it since.

I miss those simple times. The ease of just being with the person you loved—no games, no deception, no fear of judgment. We were the best of friends, and because of that, we pushed each other to succeed, even if it meant letting him grow further without me.

*How has it already been thirty years?*

"What's goin' on in that head of yours, Faye? It's been a minute, but I'm certain your wheels are spinning at Mach 1."

"I wouldn't go that far," I hedge, knowing I'm nowhere close to spinning out of control. "It's just... weird, awkward, unexpected to have you here." I never in a million years would have put running into Mark Lancaster on my bingo card, yet here we are.

Reaching out, he squeezes my hand, and instantly, I feel as if the world settles. "I get it...." Inhaling deeply, he sighs. "No need to explain."

After a few long moments, he lets go of my hand and uses it to suggest I continue eating. Nodding to me, he demands, "Eat." Then, on a low chuckle that makes my pulse race again, he adds, "It's not like I'm going anywhere."

Not. Going. Anywhere.

*Why does that simultaneously calm and unnerve me?*

But I do as I'm told.

Picking up my sandwich, I dip it into the au jus and squeeze the end quickly so I won't end up wearing it while I eat. "Mmmmm... This is good," I practically moan after chewing.

The prime rib is cooked to perfection, and my lack of eating from nerves catches up with me. Before I know it, I've completely consumed half my plate.

We watch in silence as couples fill the dance floor.

As a song ends, the lead singer talks up the crowd.

Eventually, one loud guy from the bar yells, "Got any country in you?"

Looking at his band, the lead singer's voice turns gravelly. "What do ya say, boys? Can we do country?"

The members of his band grumble among themselves for a moment, but then the drummer's sticks count off a beat, and they set into playing "Watermelon Crawl," originally by Tracy Byrd, and the crowd goes wild. Couples pile onto the floor, and I find myself tapping my toes to the beat and grinning as I watch the sudden commotion. There's a group line dancing in the center, while others partner off around the edge of the wooden floor. Some are two-stepping, others in full country swing—twisting their partners like a pretzel and flipping them like they haven't a care in the world.

When the song switches to a cover of "She Don't Know She's Beautiful," originally by Sammy Kershaw, my heart floods with memories. Back in the day, this was the song that changed everything between Mark and me.

*We'd built a fire by the beach and were leaning against each other, watching the sunset. This song was playing on the radio, and the wind was blowing my hair around like crazy. Mark had reached up and placed a piece back behind my ear, like he'd done a million times, but this time, he hesitated. His eyes caught mine and never let go.*

*We'd been flirting around things for a long time, but I could tell in that moment that a decision had been made. He was willing to cross that imaginary line we'd been skating around for months.*

*All it took was one look, and I was on board with his plan.*

*Leaning in, he never took his eyes off mine.*

*That is, until our lips brushed, and all bets were off.*

*It was one of those all-consuming kisses that you never want to break from. The kind that I'd spent months fantasizing about but was too chicken to make the first move. The kind that could only mean one thing—Our days of being "just friends" were over, and I never wanted to go back.*

Mark bumps my shoulder, breaking me out of my reverie, as he asks, "You still know how to dance to this?"

Heat floods through me as I return from memory lane.

Somehow, I manage to keep a straight face and shrug. "I might."

Holding out a hand, he says, "Let's see if we've still got it in us."

Like a moth to a flame, I let him take my hand and lead me onto the dance floor.

*Damn, he's filled out over the years.*

His strong, muscular frame leads me around as if we've been doing it for years.

I don't even remember the last time I danced on my own—let alone with anyone else—but being in his arms is far from a hardship. We drift around the floor with ease, and I pick up the moves he guides me through much quicker than I would've imagined.

As he spins me out, he catches me off guard with a new move. My feet trip on themselves, but he quickly helps me recover by pulling me close.

With his strong arms holding me tight, I'm certain he whispers, "You're still just as beautiful as ever," but I can't be sure.

"Wha..." escapes my lips as I rear back to look him in the eye, but he cuts me off.

Pointedly, with his eyes locked on mine, he states, "You heard what I said, Faye. The only difference between the first time I told you and now is that you're even more beautiful."

My stomach dips as electricity pulses through my veins, making my body react before my brain can think better of it. The next thing I know, I'm cupping his stubbled jaw and pulling him closer.

All the pent-up energy I've been holding in from the moment my eyes landed on Mark three days ago flows between us in an instant.

Without hesitation, his lips crash onto mine, and a fiery inferno explodes between us. Simultaneously, his hand slides along my back to my neck as the other pulls my hip flush against him.

My body melts into him as our kiss deepens. Heat floods through me as his tongue meets mine, making my brain short-circuit and my need for him grow out of control. Every nerve ending in my body trips like a live wire and pulses through me, from my head to my toes, with each beat of my heart.

I barely even notice when someone accidentally bumps into us, causing Mark to regretfully break our kiss.

Thank God Mark's holding me upright, or I'd be a puddle on the ground.

We barely hear the intruders' muttered "Sorry" over the music, but all I can do is stare at the sexy man before me.

Mark's eyes never leave mine as he rakes a palm over the grin I swear he's trying to hide.

"What the hell was that?" I pant as I wonder how in the world this man managed to completely consume me with just a kiss.

He smirks triumphantly, then leans in so only I can hear as he says, "That, my dear, was one hell of a kiss."

*You can say that again.*

Leaning in, he brushes his lips against mine again, then pulls back with a devilish grin as he reaches for my hand.

"I'm not so sure I'm gonna be able to keep dancing with you if you keep lookin' at me like that. What do you say, Faye? You wanna get out of here?"

Reaching up on my toes to steal one more kiss, I sigh heavily, then quickly add, "I thought you'd never ask."

# Chapter 7
## Mark

Somehow, I manage to get us home without breaking too many traffic laws.

Holy fuck, I can't believe how fast things heated up between Faye and me on that dance floor. What started as an innocent kiss kicked into overdrive in no time. If that couple hadn't bumped into us, I'm sure it would have turned indecent in only a matter of moments.

I'm always in control and never caught off guard.

How could I have allowed that to happen?

*It's Faye Ames, you dipshit.*

She's always had this effect on you.

As I pull into my driveway, I've never been more thankful for living in this small town. It took less than seven minutes to navigate home, and from the look Faye's giving me now, I'm not even sure we'll make it inside.

I kill the engine as the garage door shuts behind us, then reach across and cup her cheek, pulling her in for a kiss. Now that there's no longer an audience, I finally allow myself to get lost in her.

"Mmmm…" she groans, and it takes everything in me not to drag her across the console and onto my lap. Positioning myself into a better angle to devour her lips, the loud blaring of my horn scares the shit out of both of us.

Instantly, we jump apart.

Gasping for air, Faye places her hand on her heart as she darts her eyes around the cab.

Once she assesses the situation and realizes it was only my idiotic elbow that bumped the horn, she pats my arm and chuckles, "Wow, Rico Suave… You really know how to pull out the punches!"

"I'll show you all the punches," I challenge, unbuckling my seat belt and throwing open my door. "Wait there," I instruct, exiting the cab.

The moment I open her door and reach for her hand, she takes it without hesitation. Stepping close to help her down, she somehow simultaneously turns her legs toward me and lets her body slide along mine as she exits.

*Fuck. She feels good.*

Her hand lingers on my chest as her heated eyes bore into mine.

Needing to taste her again, I dip my head and kiss her for all I'm worth.

We may have a past, but this side of her is new.

Gone is the shy girl I shared all my firsts with.

Faye's all woman now.

From the way she's pressing her body against mine, I'm certain she knows exactly what she wants—and I'll eagerly comply.

When her fingertips dig into the hair at the base of my neck, I groan deeply.

I want to taste her—everywhere.

"Damn, Faye…" Kiss. "You…" Kiss. "Taste… incredible," I

pant, trailing kisses to that sensitive spot just under her ear that used to drive her wild.

Fuck, Faye doesn't disappoint.

The soft hitches in her breath, the tiny moans that escape, and the way her nails dig into my back only turn me on further.

I'm suddenly consumed with the combination of vanilla, lavender, and something entirely her. My body strums to life, and I can't wait to see what else turns this sexy vixen on.

Tilting her head back to get a better angle, I slip a thigh between her legs and pull her up my body.

Just as I cup her ass and haul her up to kiss her once again, I'm vaguely aware of a loud click, and the garage goes pitch dark.

I don't need lights to enjoy this beautiful woman before me, but apparently, Faye notices and immediately breaks our connection.

Suddenly, her beautiful laugh fills the room. "We certainly know how to get carried away."

"You won't hear me complaining," I tease, taking her hand and leading her through the darkness.

"Come on. Let's get inside. It's been a while, and as much as I don't mind kissing you in the dark, I'd prefer seeing that beautiful face and sexy body of yours."

Shaking her head, she grins widely. "You always were quite the charmer."

The moment we step away from my truck, the motion sensor I have must trip, and a bright light illuminates the room. In a few short steps, we enter the mudroom.

Faye gasps as she looks around at the upgrades I've made.

"Wow, if this is what your mudroom looks like, I can't wait to see the rest of your house. God knows, I've spent enough time these past few days wondering what you've done to the place."

As I watch her take in the room, I try to see it from her eyes.

Sure, I've created a nook along one side of the room for each of my grandkids to put their backpacks, coats, and shoes when they visit. There's a bench to sit on in the corner, and my washer and dryer, as well as a few cabinets for storage, line the other wall. But it was necessary to keep the chaos at bay. Kids come with a lot of crap, and unless I wanted it spread throughout my house, I needed to create a home for it.

"I'm slowly making progress," I admit, stepping closer to Faye. Leaning in, I quickly kiss that shocked expression off her lips. When I pull back, her eyes shine with mirth.

"I'd be happy to show you around," I offer with a shrug. I've still got a lot to do, but if she's impressed by this, I'm certain she'll love the rest of my plans.

Winking, she runs a finger along my sternum and smiles seductively.

This knowing look has all parts of me rising to attention.

"If anyone asks, we're gonna pretend I took the whole tour. But for now, I only care about touring *one* particular location."

"What's that?" I ask, cocking my head to the side to read her better.

I'll admit, my curiosity is piqued. I can usually judge things from a mile away, but this is Faye. She's bound to keep me on my toes.

"Your bedroom," she whispers, pulling my neck down to close the distance between us.

God, this woman is perfect.

Leaning in, I brush my lips against hers. "I think I can make that happen."

The second our lips touch, her guttural moan tells me all I need to know.

Faye and I are exactly on the same page.

# Chapter 8
## Faye

The next thing I know, Mark scoops me up, and on instinct, my legs wrap around his waist with ease. I swear it's like he was made for me, and we fit together perfectly. I haven't been carried like this by anyone but him in my entire life.

I feel young and carefree again.

Logically, I know a lot has changed in thirty years, but we can deal with what that means later.

All that matters in this moment is experiencing whatever *this* is between us.

Maybe if I give in and just let things happen, I'll get him out of my system and finally be able to concentrate on *anything* other than Mark again.

As his hands grip my ass tighter, his tongue delves deeper, making my entire body hum with desire, and all contemplation of what-ifs disappears.

As my hands roam his muscular chest, a thought hits me like a ton of bricks—holy hell, this man must work out like crazy. Not only is he kissing the ever-living shit out of me, but he ascends the freaking stairs as if I'm a Velcro monkey rather than the grown-ass woman who's certainly changed since being a gangly teen.

Who does this?

*Mark Lancaster, apparently.*

My body pulses with need with each step we travel.

He's hotter than any book boyfriend or fantasy I could've imagined.

His kisses burn me from the inside out. Every nip, suck, and stroke of his tongue possessively consumes my every thought.

I need more.

I'm vaguely aware of rooms passing by as we travel through the house, but it isn't until he stops moving that I notice we've arrived in his bedroom.

When the hand that's gripping my ass and holding me in place glides up my back, I take it as my cue to release my legs from his waist.

Sliding down his body for the second time tonight in slow motion, I feel every sculpted muscle hidden beneath his thin T-shirt.

"Damn, you feel amazing." The compliment slips from his lips as his large hand slides under my shirt, then trails up my spine, making me tingle from head to toe.

Laughing, I admit, "You took the words right out of my mouth."

Running my hands along his pecks, my need to lick every square inch of his chest has me clawing at the shirt tucked into his black cargo pants.

When Mark steps back, I almost cry at the loss of contact.

Reaching one arm over his shoulder, he quickly tugs at his shirt and removes it in one fluid motion.

My mouth feels drier than the sand in any desert as my eyes roam his body.

Holy fucking shit. Mark's been holding out on me.

*How on earth has he gotten so much better-looking with age?*

If I thought he was hot before, he's like a fucking Greek god now.

His muscles are sculpted to perfection. A smattering of dark hair covers his chest, and oh, my freaking god, where did that V come from? He never had anything like that when we were kids.

I've never seen anything like this other than on cover models or in the movies. This doesn't happen in real life.

We're freaking forty-eight. Isn't he supposed to have a dad bod or something like that? It takes everything in me not to stick out my finger and poke him, just to ensure I haven't completely conjured him in my mind.

For fuck's sake, I wouldn't put it past my imagination.

After all, he's all I've been able to think about for days.

When my eyes drift down to peruse the large bulge in his pants, the loud clearing of his throat fills the room. "Eyes up here, sweetheart."

The old me would have been embarrassed to be so blatantly checking him out.

But not this time.

I'm proudly enjoying every moment.

Purposely, I take my time dragging my eyes to his.

It's obvious he's worked hard on his body, and I'm not ashamed that I'm simply appreciating his efforts.

When our eyes finally meet, I'm not prepared for the heat searing at me.

The desire and need in that one look nearly incinerates me on the spot.

Who knows how long I stare, but eventually, an uneven grin forms on his lips as he reaches for the hem of my shirt.

"If you're gonna keep lookin' at me like that, there's no way I'll be able to take things slow." His sexy voice is low and gravelly and does something to me that I can't quite explain.

"Who said we need to take things slow?"

As if I haven't just poured gasoline on this fire between us, I reach for the hem of my shirt and pull it over my head with ease.

I've never been more thankful for stopping in that French lingerie shop on my last trip to Paris than I am in this moment. If I thought Mark's gaze was heated before, his dark hazel eyes might melt my royal-blue satin two-piece set without even touching me.

A guttural moan escapes his lips as he reaches for my hip and tugs me closer. "You're gonna be the death of me, Faye, if you keep teasing me like that."

"Oh, I'm not teasing," I promise.

Leaning down, he brushes a kiss against my swollen lips. "Good. Now... let's get these pants off you so I can see if my hunch is right."

"What's that?" I ask, having no idea where he's going with this.

Giving my ass a quick squeeze, he smirks. "I'm dying to know if you're still in the habit of wearing matching underwear."

"Guess you'll have to see for yourself," I tease, untying the drawstring of my joggers.

Before I can push them down, Mark reaches for me and slips his thumbs into my waistband to help me glide them over my hips.

As I shimmy them off and toe them aside, Mark's guttural groan fills the room.

"Mmmm... Faye. You're so fuckin' sexy."

Feeling bold, I step back and slowly spin to let him appreciate all aspects of the blue panties he was eager to see. They give me full coverage in the front, but the back is a no-show thong, leaving my cheeks exposed.

His quick intake of breath lets me know my newfound hobby is a success.

*Who knew going to the gym to help Dad get back into shape would have so many benefits for me?*

Mark always was an ass man, and from the look in his eyes that meet mine when I face him, I'm glad to see some things haven't changed.

"You're playing with fire, Faye," is the only warning I get.

Before inhaling my next breath, he reaches for me and crashes his lips onto mine.

This time, as he palms my ass and lifts me off my feet, he merely pivots and drops me onto the enormous king-sized bed behind us.

Eager for him to join me, I scooch toward the center of his dark-gray comforter, but he stops me with a hand on my calf. "Not so fast, sweetheart. I've spent the better part of three days fantasizing about you... Not to mention it's been over thirty years since we've been together. There's no way in hell we're rushing this."

For the second time tonight, my heart squeezes at the memories.

He's the only one who's ever called me sweetheart—well, the only one I ever let get away with it.

With Mark, it was never derogatory or condescending.

It was truly a form of endearment.

One that held hope and the promise of a future.

One that made me feel safe and confident to just be myself.

I never had to be anything but me when we were together.

Maybe it's because he was my first, but there was something different about the way we explored one another and pushed things to the next level that always had me burning with desire and ready to go when it came to him.

Mark interrupts my trip down memory lane by running a palm along my inner leg up to my thigh and down to my ankle.

Tugging me to the end of the bed, he lets out a low whistle. "Damn, your skin is just as smooth as I remember," he murmurs.

Goose bumps scatter across my heated flesh as my core clenches.

Brushing his lips along my calf, he moans in satisfaction. "Fuck, you taste just like I remember."

"What do you mean?" The question flies from my mouth before I can think better of it.

Between kisses up my leg, he satisfies my curiosity.

"Fuck... You taste like a warm summer day.... I swear there's a hint of vanilla and lavender..." He stops to run his tongue along my inner thigh, and it takes everything in me not to squirm like crazy.

"But it's so much more than that... You just taste like..." He shakes his head as if he can't find the words, and I feel his hot breath at the apex of my thighs.

"God, that feels good," I cry, fisting the soft comforter beneath me.

Licking his tongue along my skin just beneath the seam of my panties, my hips buck into him, and he finally continues his thought on an exhale. "Like you."

I barely process his words when his finger slides beneath the fabric along my other thigh. It glides with ease through my folds and circles my clit, only to slide into me and stroke me from within.

"Oh, Mark... Right there," I encourage as he sets a steady rhythm that will have me coming in record time.

When he adds another digit, I can barely form a coherent thought.

It feels beyond words.

He touches me in ways my vibrator never can. It's been way too long since any man has made me feel like this. Threading my fingers through his hair, I guide him to where I want him most.

Unfortunately, instead of doing what I need, his body shifts, and his fingers withdraw.

"Fuck... Don't stop..." I plead in protest.

"Have to," he demands. "These panties are way too sexy to rip to shreds, and I need to taste this beautiful pussy of yours."

"Well... *That* I can get on board with." I laugh. "I am quite fond of them."

"You and me both, sweetheart."

Lifting my hips, he quickly assists me in removing them. "Besides... You'd have to take me to Paris to get more."

"Hmmm..." he ponders as he comes up to cup my cheek, then brushes a tender kiss over my lips. "We never did get to travel. You still got that bucket list we made as kids?"

"I've checked a few things off over the years," I admit with a smirk. "But you know me, I'm always adding to it."

Holding my gaze, one hand braces himself above me on the bed, while the other returns to stroke my clit. "I can think of a few things I'd like to add to mine."

"What's... that?" I ask, but my breath hitches when he presses his fingers deep inside me.

Leaning in, he kisses me once more.

When he pulls back, his challenging smirk that always had me pushing my limits makes an appearance. "I think I'd rather show you the most important item on my list. We can get to the rest later."

Without a word, he kisses down my body.

His heated breath feels amazing on my skin. His rough whiskers leave a tantalizing sensation and have me begging for more. While he fingers me with one hand, the other pulls the cups of my bra down. When my boobs spring free, he wastes no time trailing kisses from one nipple to the other.

I'm on sensation overload as three incredible things happen at once. One hand slowly slides in and out of my dripping-wet pussy, the other plumps my breast and rolls a thumb over a rock-hard peak, while his wicked mouth sucks my other nipple into his mouth and tugs lightly with his teeth.

An appreciative moan escapes. "Oh... My... Fucking... Mark! What are you doing to me?"

I feel the rumble of his laughter before hearing it. "Somebody still loves nipple play, I see."

"Suck like that again... Fuck... It feels incredible."

I'm so close to coming, it's not even funny.

My core clenches around his fingers, and Mark must feel it because suddenly, his laughter fills the room again. "I've barely touched you, Faye. Need me to slow down?"

"Not on your fucking life," I pant. "If you stop... I might... Die."

"Well, we wouldn't want that, now, would we?" He chortles huskily. Trailing kisses along my ribs, he quickly adds, "But... I might die if I don't taste that sweet pussy of yours."

That's the only warning I get.

As his finger still strokes my inner walls, he shifts his body so his shoulders wedge between my thighs.

"I could get on board with that," I muse, running my fingers into his hair to guide him where I need him most.

I should've known better.

Mark needs no direction in navigating my nether regions.

Using his thumbs to part my folds, he languidly licks me from my core to my clit, and I nearly rocket off the bed.

Pressing a palm on my abdomen to hold me in place, he taunts, "You like that, do you?" Without waiting for a response, he quickly repeats his movements.

I'll assume that's a rhetorical question, because my senses are so overloaded, I can barely think words, let alone form them.

Fisting my hands into his hair, my body bucks to meet him stroke for stroke.

Electric sparks start deep in my spine and splinter through every fiber of my being, making this the most explosive orgasm I've ever experienced in my life.

My body flashes with heat, my vision goes black, and all I can do is hold on and revel in wave after wave of ecstasy.

*Holy fucking shit, what is Mark doing to me?*

He's relentless and doesn't stop until my body stills, and my bones feel as if they've been replaced by jelly.

Lifeless, I lie on the bed, eyes closed, wondering if I'll ever be able to move again.

I'm vaguely aware of him climbing up the bed beside me.

I feel Mark prop himself onto his side as his fingers stroke across my skin.

When the backside of his fingers slides along my jaw, he finally speaks, "You okay over there?"

"Shhh... Feels too good to move," I hiss, not wanting to leave this state of consciousness.

My eyes might as well be superglued together, and my limbs are like bricks. If I die, this is truly the best way to go.

His sexy chuckle fills the room. "I think I can find a way to make you feel even better."

Now, this has my attention.

Slowly, I force myself to face him and pry my eyes open.

"Really? You think you can top that?"

"Oh, Faye. You have no idea what I can do," he says, bringing his mouth to mine.

The touch of our lips brings a spark of energy back to me.

Rolling to my side to face him, my hard nipples brush against his broad chest.

Needing him closer, I run my hand along his back and pull myself flush against him. When my fingers trail along his belt, I declare, "You have entirely too many clothes on, Lancaster."

"Hmm... I think I can remedy that."

Within seconds, he's standing at the base of the bed, toeing off his shoes and unbuckling his belt. Needing in on the action, I fly across the mattress on my knees to assist him. My fingers make it just in time to help him push his cargo pants over his hips, leaving him standing only in black boxer briefs.

This man is a sight to be seen.

My eyes never leave his as I reach behind my back.

Unhooking my bra, I slowly remove it and drop it on the floor beside us in a challenge.

For the longest time, we wordlessly stare at one another as the energy crackles between us. All that we hear is our heavy breathing and the blood pulsing through my ears as my heart thunders.

Mark breaks the silence when he hooks his thumbs in his boxers, pushes them off his hips, then says, "You're so fucking beautiful, sweetheart."

My pulse skyrockets as I watch his thick cock spring to life.

Reaching down, he tugs it twice as if internally telling it to behave.

But I've got other ideas for that sexy cock of his.

Reaching to cup his balls, my eyes return to his, and I squeeze him gently. "It's my turn to taste you."

"Later, sweetheart. Like you, I'm already teetering on the

edge, and there's no chance in hell I'm coming anywhere other than in that sweet pussy of yours."

With that, he leans in and crushes his lips to mine, and I'm lost in all things Mark.

I'm vaguely aware of being pushed back onto the bed and dragged up to the pillows. Every nip, suck, and grunt that comes from my body brings me further to life. I need this man more than I need my next breath.

When his body aligns with mine, he pants, "Condom?"

I know I'm safe, and there's absolutely zero chance of pregnancy, but I'm not ready to get into that with him now. Mark's the only one I'm dying to feel all of, but fuck, we're not ready for that conversation. It would be a total buzzkill.

Instead, I say, "I'm clean and protected. If you think we need one, then use it."

"You sure? Since my divorce, I've always used condoms. I was tested just before I left the Air Force, and I haven't been with anyone since."

"But that was..." I start, trying to do the math.

"Even longer than that," he admits. "Other than when I was married, I've always used condoms, Faye. And you know how long ago I got divorced."

"I've never gone without one," I admit.

Mark's eyes go round as saucers, "Never?"

"Never."

Thankfully, my gut instinct was right about Corey. In this moment, it's never been clearer that I never trusted him, even after all those years of being together. Even after all our time apart, I somehow trust Mark implicitly.

Mark's lips purse, and I can tell he's thinking about something.

Just as I'm about to call him on it, his face breaks out into the sexiest of smiles. "Can I have another of your firsts, then?"

*Firsts? What's he talking about?*

Then it hits me, and I can't help the grin that forms.

We were each other's first everything.

"It wouldn't be right with anyone but you, Mark."

Pressing his lips to mine, I can hear the smile in his voice. "Glad to know we're on the same page."

Knowing I'm more than ready for him, I reach for his bobbing cock and squeeze him gently.

"Fuck, Faye. Stop teasing," Mark demands. "Let me feel you."

Not wanting to waste another minute, I drop my knees open further as I line him up with my entrance. The moment he presses against me, I'm reminded of just how much our bodies have changed. Gone is the boy who fumbled around, exploring every inch of my body as a teen. In his place is a man who knows exactly what he's doing.

There's nothing timid in the way Mark's kisses completely consume me.

As if he's got all the time in the world, he slowly works his cock into my tight channel bit by bit, letting my body adjust as he goes.

Once he's fully seated, he groans, "Fuck, you feel incredible."

Needing to move, I beg, "Mmmm... More, Mark."

Mark slowly pulls out almost to the tip, then thrusts back in.

It hits the perfect spot. "Oh... Fuck... Right there."

Gripping his ass, I pull him close. "Faster, Mark. I need you."

What starts as slow, languid thrusts turns into a fiery frenzy.

We're nothing but tongues, teeth, and carnal need. The way his hips piston into me, I truly can't get enough. I'm teetering on the edge of another orgasm in a matter of minutes.

Without warning, Mark flips us over and demands, "Ride me."

Pressing my hands onto his chest for balance, I quickly find a rhythm.

Reaching for my breasts, he pulls and plays with my nipples.

"God, Faye... You're phenomenal," he pants as I grind my pelvic bone against his.

"Oh... Right there, Mark," I plead when he pinches my nipple, and electricity zips through my spine. "That feels... so... good."

My core clenches when Mark's sexy voice fills the room. "Fuck... You're even more responsive than I remember."

"I blame you," I admit, grinding on him. "You feel so fucking good."

"I blame us," he says as he thrusts from below me.

Even from the bottom, he's taking control.

But I'll never complain.

At this angle, his cock hits me in a place only he has ever reached.

When he cups my breast and rolls my nipple between his fingers, the earth shatters beneath me. Sparks of energy break from my core and pulse through every nerve ending of my body.

As I spasm around his cock, I feel Mark thrust into me faster.

Once, twice, three times.

On the fourth, he reaches for my hips and grinds me onto his cock, pressing deeper than before.

His loud groan fills the room, and through my tremors, I feel him release into me. Wrapping my arms around his body, I squeeze his pulsing cock as long as I can, never wanting this moment between us to end.

Eventually, our bodies relax into one another.

If I thought I was boneless before, I was sadly mistaken.

Listening to the steady beat of his heart as I lay my head against his chest, my limbs feel like lead weights, and the only thing I'm aware of is how perfect it feels to be in his arms.

Stroking my hair down my back, Mark eventually breaks the silence. "You still with me?"

"Barely," I confess. "That was..." I trail off, fighting to find the words.

"Unlike anything I've experienced before."

Thankfully, he takes the words right out of my mouth.

"That was definitely one of my best firsts," I admit. "You always did know how to take things to the next level."

"There's no one else I'd rather share my firsts with than you."

# Chapter 9
## Mark

Waking up to the feel of Faye's lips wrap around my cock is something I never knew I needed until this morning.

Talk about a wake-up call. Fuck, this woman is insatiable, and I'm here for it.

"Hmmmm... Good morning," I moan, fisting my hand into her soft blonde hair.

When her beautiful blue eyes meet mine, my heart skips a beat.

She gives me a knowing smirk and mumbles something that sounds like a greeting. However, with her mouth otherwise occupied, I don't understand her exact words.

Even though I came only a few hours ago, my dick clearly didn't get the message that we're supposed to be sated. He's roaring and ready to start the day off right. Watching Faye fist the base and pump along my length as her tongue swirls around the tip only makes him grow bigger.

When she cups my balls and presses the sensitive skin behind them with one hand, as she strokes me with the other, I nearly rocket off the bed. Throw in watching those sexy pink lips sucking me off, and I may as well just die and go to heaven.

"Fuuuck..." I groan in satisfaction, and my need to make her feel just as good intensifies. "Why don't you come up here and let me satisfy both of us?"

With a shake of her head, she moans and doubles down on her efforts.

I should've known better. This woman loves a challenge.

Before I know it, I'm on the brink of blowing my load.

"I..." I gasp. "I'm already close."

Faye doesn't say anything but simply squeezes me tighter as her head bobs faster.

As I barrel toward the point of no return, I warn with desperation, "Pull off, Faye. I'm about to..."

Her cheeks hollow out and suck even harder as this sexy vixen presses firmer on that spot that drives me crazy.

That's all it takes.

Pulse after pulse, I explode into her.

She sucks and strokes until I truly can't take it any longer.

Tugging her off my cock, I plead, "Too sensitive."

Running the back of her palm over her lips, a wicked grin forms. "You didn't let me use that as an excuse when you went down on me a few hours ago." Arching a brow, she asks, "Why should I let you use it now?"

"Women are made for multiples," I point out. "Men... Not so much. I need a bit of time to recover."

Pulling her up to snuggle against my chest, a light laugh escapes. "Fair point."

Glancing at the clock, I'm shocked to see it's nearly seven.

"Have you been up long?"

"Not really." Pointing to my cock, she grins, "He woke me up with an apparent need to come out and play."

"It's a dick. They do that," I deadpan. Running a hand up

her spine, I add, "I find if you just ignore it, it'll settle down if you don't want it."

Running a finger along my pecks, she says, "Oh, I wanted. You were stingy last night and never let me taste you."

"I was rather preoccupied," I point out. "Besides," I add, kissing her temple, "you taste better."

Before she can reply, my phone rings from the pocket of my jeans.

Knowing it's likely one of the girls, I scramble to the end of the bed in search of where I left it.

Fishing it out of my pocket, I see the caller and apologize to Faye. "Sorry. This is Sloane."

Pulling the blanket closer to her chest, she shrugs. "Take it. I don't mind."

On the fourth ring, I crawl back up the bed to sit beside her and answer, "Hey, Sloane," as I settle against my headboard.

"Hey, Dad." From her tone alone, I sense something is up.

"What's going on?" I ask, sitting straighter.

Sloane lets out a huff of frustration. "Jax just had to change his flight from LA this afternoon, and I'm due to fly out to New York in a few hours."

"Okay..." I draw out. That doesn't seem this stressful.

Then she adds, "And my sitter just cancelled due to a family emergency. Any chance you can watch the boys until Jax returns?"

"Uhhh..." I draw out as disappointment sets in. There goes any plans I could've made with Faye today.

Giving Faye an apologetic smile, I return my attention to the phone. "Sure... I'll uh... Just need to shower and get ready. Want me to pick them up from your place in about an hour?"

"Shower?" Sloane's voice rises as if I just told her I had three heads.

"Yeah... I... Uh... got a late start this morning," I admit.

Reaching for Faye's hand, I mouth, *"Sorry,"* to assure her I'm not blowing her off.

"Oh, my... Has hell frozen over?" Sloane sputters in disbelief.

Faye must hear her because she covers her mouth to hold back a laugh.

"Shut it, smartass!" There's no way in hell I'm telling my daughter why I'm still in bed at this hour, so I do what I do best: deflect. "If you want my help, it's best you stop picking on me. How long will you need me to watch the twins?"

Regardless of how long she needs, Sloane knows she can count on me.

After my retirement, I vowed to myself to make up for lost time. If given a choice, I will always be here when my girls need me most. That's the entire reason I returned to Seaside in the first place.

"Uh..." Sloane draws out, and I can hear the wheels spinning in her head as she mentally goes through their crazy schedules. She's working her way up the chain at the record label. Thanks to her and Jax's talent, his band, Ruby Frax, keeps topping the charts, and they're as popular as ever.

"Jax and the guys' music video got delayed due to weather. He should be home by tomorrow, or the next day, tops. I'm meeting with a new artist in New York after catching them live at their concert tomorrow night, then following up with another the next day. If we weren't so close to the music festival here in Seaside next month, I'd cancel my trip. But I'd really like this act to perform."

"I've got you," I assure her. "I'll pick the boys up and bring them to my place. You just take your time and do what you need to do back east."

"Thanks, Dad." She sighs heavily into the phone. "I don't know what I'd do without you."

"Oh, you'd manage," I assure her. That girl has always been so goal-driven. She has more determination in her little toe than people have in a lifetime. If she so much as thinks it, Sloane will find a way to make her desires happen.

"What about Raven? Will she need help on the home front if Finn's stuck in LA?"

"I don't think so. Her girls have a special day camp this week for dance, and she's been working from home. She's got a big design she's working on, so I'm sure she's busy with that, but it's nothing too out of the ordinary."

"I'll reach out and see how things are doing later today. Maybe I'll invite them over for some cousin time this evening."

"You know if you do that, you'll end up with the whole lot of them, right?" Sloane warns with a laugh. "Only you don't get to send Jason and Josh home after you've wound them up."

Her boys are spunky and full of energy as it is, but I'll never turn down any time I get with my grandchildren. "I've commanded thousands of airmen. I'm sure I can handle my rowdy squadron."

"Ha..." she snorts loudly into the phone. "But your troops never batted their eyelashes or had you wrapped around their fingers. I swear, my boys practically get away with murder, compared to what you let us do as kids."

This time, Faye can't contain her low laughter.

Christ, I can't win for losing on this front.

Rolling my eyes, I quickly spit out, "Hey now... Don't be kickin' a gift horse in the mouth," I warn. "If you want me there within the hour, I'd better get movin'."

"Okay... Okay..." Sloane's laughter is barely contained. "I still can't believe you're not up and moving. This must be a record for you to sleep in this late."

Looking at Faye, who's giving me the *she's got you there* look, I can only shake my head.

My silence prompts Sloane to playfully add, "I wonder if pigs are flying somewhere."

Locking eyes with my reason for letting Sloane get the best of me, I shrug. "Miracles do happen." Before Sloane can make anything of it, I quickly add, "See you in a bit, Sloane. Tell Jax I've got you both covered and to just take care of business."

"Love you, Dad." She sighs into the phone.

"Love you, too, kiddo. Now, get moving." Not sure which of us needs that reminder more, but as I look at Faye, I'm hoping I can make some of the next hour count.

With a laugh, Sloane disconnects the call.

Turning my attention to the beautiful woman beside me, I give her by best apologetic smile. "Sorry about that."

"There's nothing to be sorry for, Mark."

"I was hoping to spend more time with you today," I admit.

"It's not a problem." Reaching for my hand, she quickly squeezes it. "Besides, some of us aren't retired and still have to work."

"Can I at least make you some breakfast before I go?" I offer as consolation.

Glancing at the clock, she asks, "Do you have time?"

"It might not be elaborate, but I can whip us up some eggs and toast."

"What about a shower?" she points out.

"As in you'd rather shower than eat?" I could get on board with that.

Shoving my shoulder, she sighs. "No, you insatiable fool... You and I both know if we showered together, there's no way you'll get there on time. I meant, do *you* need to shower?"

"That takes seven minutes, tops," I point out.

Rolling her eyes, she snorts. "You are such a guy."

"That includes getting dressed," I add for good measure, puffing out my chest.

"Yeah... I could never do that."

"I'll tell you what... You go shower, and I'll get dressed. Is there another bathroom I could use to freshen up in?"

Standing, I head to my dresser to grab my clothes for the day. "Since I didn't really get around to giving you a proper tour of the place, you can use this one and do whatever you need, and I'll use the one down the hall. If you turn right out of my door, it will lead you to the stairs. I'll meet you in the kitchen. Coffee is on a timer, so help yourself to some if I'm not there when you arrive."

Needing to taste this gorgeous woman again, I quickly return to where she's propped against the headboard and kiss her once more.

Well, that was my intention.

The moment our lips touch, desire rushes through me, and it feels as if I'm kissing her for the first time all over again. It doesn't matter that we spent the entire night exploring every inch of one another, and I lost track of how many times we made each other come. My need for her is stronger than ever. It's like she's put a spell on me, and all sense of the world beyond us disappears.

In all too short a time, she breaks our kiss, and her beautiful laughter fills the room.

When I reach for her again, she shoves me toward the door. "Go. You keep this up, and your daughter's likely to show up looking for you. We'll never get dressed at this rate."

"There could be worse things," I grumble, feigning rejection.

She's got a point, but it doesn't mean I have to like it.

"If you think I'm meeting your daughter and grandkids for the first time *naked*, in your bed, Lancaster, you've got another thing coming."

"God, you're adorable when you're feisty," I admit, pecking

her on the nose. "Though you got a point. That would certainly be traumatizing... For everyone involved. I'll meet you downstairs for breakfast, sweetheart. Take your time."

———

SIX AND A HALF MINUTES LATER, I'm dressed and downstairs, pulling two mugs from the cupboard and filling them with coffee. A pan is warming on the stove, but Faye has yet to make an appearance. There's water running, so I know she's still upstairs.

As I'm bent over, rummaging in the fridge and reaching for the eggs, I hear an amused, "How the hell did you do that?"

Turning, I quickly ask for clarification. "Do what?"

With my hands full of milk and eggs, I elbow the door shut behind me and step to the counter to place what I need by the stove.

"Beat me down here." Shaking her head, she adds, "I swear, it wasn't even ten minutes."

"I've got places to be." I shrug. "Besides, why would I waste time in the shower when I can spend more time with you?"

Ignoring her adorable eye roll, I point at her coffee. "You still take it with cream and sugar?"

Sighing heavily, she nods and sits at the counter in front of the cup and sugar dispenser I've set out for her. "How do you remember that? It's been thirty years."

Handing her the milk in my hands, I shrug. "Sweetheart, I'm sure there are plenty of things to still learn, trust me." Just as she's about to pour, I remember. "Oh, the girls like flavored creamer. I think there might be caramel or vanilla creamer in the door if you're interested."

"This is fine. Thanks." She pours a dash of sugar and milk into the mug. Once she's done, she cups it and brings it to her mouth for a taste. "Mmmmm... I'm gonna need this today." When her eyes find mine, she asks, "Want any help?"

"Nope. I got this. Just relax."

While she enjoys her coffee, I make quick work by plopping our toast into the toaster and making sure the skillet is ready. Just as I'm about to crack her eggs, I ask for reassurance, "You still like your eggs over easy?"

From the corner of my eye, I catch her jaw drop, and she stares wordlessly for a few beats before shaking her head and replying, "Yep, I sure do."

Cracking the egg with one hand, I ask, "What are your plans today?"

Her eyes look to the ceiling, and she ticks items off her fingers. "I need to hop on a call at ten, then another at one, and I'm working on a few projects that will take most of the day."

With her line of work, I know better than to pry for further details, so instead, I change the subject. "Any idea when you think you'll be done?"

"Well..." She sighs heavily and glances at her watch. "Since I'm getting a late start, and I have back-to-back meetings this afternoon, I'm not sure."

The toast pops up, and I reach to plate it. Before I put anything on hers, I ask, "Butter?"

"Yes, please."

Once that's done, I return to the stove and flip the eggs, then gather our silverware. In a matter of minutes, our breakfast is done, and I'm sitting beside her on a barstool.

"Was the place like this when you moved in?" she asks, glancing around my open-concept living room and kitchen.

"I hired a company to replace the windows and repaint the outside while I tinkered on projects like renovating the downstairs bathroom and upgrading this kitchen. Thankfully, the wood floors were in great shape throughout the house, and the former owners repainted most of the interior before selling—though there are a few rooms I'd like to change up, but I'll get there."

"It's lookin' good." She nods, then takes another bite. When she's finished chewing, she adds, "I always wondered what this place looked like inside. I think it was vacant for a while before you moved in... Or they just never used it because I haven't seen anyone since I moved in next door."

"Thankfully, it's in good-enough shape," I admit. "I don't mind a project now and then. There are still a few things that'll keep me busy for a while but nothing too pressing. The 90s kitchen has been upgraded, and for the most part, the house is livable. I just couldn't stand the dark-wood cabinets or the hunter-green countertops and single black sink."

Covering her mouth, she cackles. "No. I couldn't do that either. This kitchen is a dream. It's got plenty of space for a big family like yours. I love how bright and open it is. Not to mention it's completely functional."

As I take in this space through her eyes, I'm proud of my accomplishments. Not only did I install a large double sink that you can finally wash large dishes in, but I've also created more seating by extending the granite countertop to easily seat six around it on barstools. I also purchased a large table with long benches along the sides so we can fit more around the table than we could with chairs.

"Space was a huge selling point. I've spent too much time away over the years not to have a place we can gather. Sure, we've still got Mom's house, but all my girls are in the thick of things, raising their families. It's great for them to take a break away from their own chaos and let someone else host."

Raising a brow, Faye skeptically asks, "So, you cook more than breakfast?"

"Do you think Jane Lancaster would've let me get away

with not learning?" I ask incredulously. She should know better. Mom was adamant that my sister Mable and I learned everything we could so we could fend for ourselves. Hell, Mom made sure of that long before I even considered enlisting in the Air Force.

*Maybe I never showed Faye.*

Shaking her head, a smile tugs at her lips. "Fair point."

"Besides, a man's gotta eat. I could only take chow halls for so long. The moment I got a place of my own, I always made the most of it."

"Makes sense," Faye muses. "I'll admit I'm more of a functional cook. With my crazy schedule and it being just me, I don't waste a lot of time on anything elaborate."

"Nothing wrong with that." I feel the need to reach out and squeeze her thigh with my free hand. "Speaking of eating, got any plans this evening?"

"Like I said, I'm working most of the day. I haven't thought that far."

"I'm grilling steaks with the boys. If you're free, you're welcome to join us. If you're busy, we can drop it off."

"Oh, that's not necessary," she quickly spits out. "You should spend this time with your grandkids."

I study her carefully, trying to decipher if she's just being polite or truly uninterested in meeting my family.

"You gotta eat, don't you?" I quickly counter.

Not sure why my gut's telling me the truth behind her response matters, but for some reason, it feels important. We're neighbors; it's not like she's really going anywhere. Knowing my gut never steers me wrong, I change tactics and soften my tone. "Look, Faye, there's nothing wrong with being neighborly."

"Is that what this is?" She points between the two of us and smirks adorably. "Neighborly?"

"Fuck... Last night was..." I draw out, running a palm down my face to keep from smiling at the memory as I search for the correct words.

Hell, it was fucking phenomenal, out of this world, one of the best fucking nights of my existence. But what comes out is, "Nowhere near neighborly."

"I'd be a little jealous if you gave Mrs. Rimer, the woman who lives on the other side of you, the same treatment."

"I can assure you, you're the only neighbor I've experienced anything like last night with." To prove my point, I lean in and kiss that gorgeous smirk right off her face.

Fuck, she's addicting. If I don't keep myself in check, I'll never make it to Sloane's today.

"Good." She sighs when I pull back. "Because she's a much better cook, and I wouldn't want the competition."

"Faye, I've met Mrs. Rimer. That woman could be my grandmother," I deadpan, then put a finger beneath her chin to draw her eyes to mine. "So we're clear, you're the only one in this entire town who could tempt me to do the things I did to you last night."

"Glad to see we're on the same page," she murmurs, pulling me in for another scorching kiss.

"Oh, we're on the same page, Faye," I murmur between hot kisses.

*The bigger question is—what does this mean beyond last night?*

# Chapter 10
## Sisters Group Chat

SLOANE:

Ohmigod. I swear hell has frozen over.

RAVEN:

What's going on? You good?

SLOANE:

I called Dad at 7 a.m., and he was still sleeping. (shocked face emoji)

LIZZY:

No way!

LANIE:

You sure? Dad's up at the ass crack of dawn, every day that ends in "Y."

SLOANE:

No joke. I called because Ruby Frax is delayed in LA, and our sitter cancelled at the last minute. It was barely seven. Dad's always up, so I didn't worry about waking him.

RAVEN:

You could've called me.

SLOANE:

Not the point, Rave. I swear, he was STILL IN BED!!! His voice was gruff, and he said he still needed to shower AND that it would take him nearly an hour to get here.

LIZZY:

Dad showers in 10 min, and you live like 5 min away?!?!?!

SLOANE:

I KNOW! (head exploding emoji).

RAVEN:

Why would it take him an hour? (thinking emoji)

LANIE:

You sure he just isn't busy?

SLOANE:

He said he got a late start this morning. Clearly—he was in bed at 7 a.m.!!!

LANIE:

(Pigs flying GIF)

LIZZY:

LMAO. Is the world ending? (Head exploding GIF)

RAVEN:

It's nearly 8. Are you telling me he's not there yet?

SLOANE:

Nope. His location shows he's still at home.

LIZZY:

I'm surprised his location is back on. Wasn't he working for Riggs this week?

SLOANE:

I got a notification he was home yesterday evening.

LANIE:

Stalker much?

RAVEN:

What goes around comes around. Think about all those times he threatened to track us as kids. Someone's got to keep tabs on that man. He may be retired, but he's always up to something.

LANIE:

He probably had trackers on us as some sort of government experiment—before it became a popular app feature. Even from half a world away, he always knew what we were up to.

LIZZY:

No kidding. I couldn't get away with anything.

SLOANE:

I blame Raven. She loved pushing the envelope.

RAVEN:

Just because I wasn't a goody two-shoes like you, doesn't mean I was up to something.

LANIE:

Yeah, right. (eye roll emoji)

LIZZY:

Do you hear yourself?

SLOANE:

(arrows pointing up) Love you, Rave, but you were exactly the reason he tracked us all!

LIZZY:

As the youngest, I never stood a chance.

LANIE:

Fair point, Liz.

RAVEN:

I just got a notification that he left home.

LANIE:

You know he'd kick your ass if he knew you tracked his every move.

RAVEN:

I only set up notifications to see if he's home. It's not like the rest of you don't have your app set up like that either (for any of us).

LIZZY:

Guilty as charged. (shrugging emoji)

SLOANE:

Gotta run. My flight for NYC leaves in a few hours, and my boys are done eating breakfast.

RAVEN:

Let us know if you need anything.

SLOANE:

Will do. But I think Dad's got it covered. Tell the girls I hope they have fun at dance this week!

RAVEN:

Safe travels. Love you. (heart emoji)

LANIE:

Love you. (heart emoji)

LIZ:

Let us know when you land. (blowing
kisses gif)

SLOANE:

Love you all. Talk soon. (heart emoji)

# Chapter 11
## Mark

"Hey, Jay, slow down. Give Josh a chance to catch up," I holler, jogging to keep up with my five-year-old grandsons. Jason and his twin brother, Josh, have more bounce on them than a rubber ball. They've got two speeds, high gear and dead asleep. I know for a fact that Sloane and Jax stay busy taking care of these two.

I love the living hell out of them and wouldn't change their spunkiness for the world. But I also know my limits and have quickly learned that exercise and organized activities are key to successful overnight grandparenting. To wear them out, I've taken them longboarding along the promenade. They're really getting good since they got their boards. I have my own at home, but since they're still a bit chaotic when they ride, I thought it better not to bring mine today.

"Look at me, Papa!" Josh pumps hard with his feet and coasts around his brother with ease. With his hands behind his back, he glides down the pavement like he was made to skate.

"Way to go!" I encourage, then internally chuckle when Jason decides he isn't having it.

Pumping his leg harder, he picks up speed and zooms right up along his brother in no time.

*Ohmigod, sibling rivalry runs deep in our family.*

Their mom has always been competitive.

When Sloane sets her mind to something, there's no stopping her.

Our family jokes it's her tenacity that landed her their dad.

As an up-and-coming talent scout, she not only found Jax in a local dive bar but also introduced him to the world, and he quickly became the renowned rockstar everyone knows and loves today. From what I've learned about Jax over the years, he's just as driven. As the lead man for Ruby Frax, their band continues to top the charts with each new album. With parents like Sloane and Jax, these boys come by their competitiveness honestly. They never stood a chance.

Sprinting to catch up, I arrive just in time to overhear, "Bro, that was sick," fly out of Josh's mouth.

*These kids kill me.*

They sound more like teens than two boys barely out of toddlerhood.

I'm not responsible for their mouths, but I'll proudly take full credit for teaching them to longboard last summer. It started when I took them riding when they were barely able to walk each time I came home to visit. I've done it with all my grandkids. But I swear, these boys were naturals once they got their own boards and could practice regularly.

One good thing that came from growing up in this tiny beach town and living on the edge of the promenade was longboarding. Before I discovered girls, it was how I spent every waking moment as a kid—well, that and surfing. But I'm not ready to teach my grandkids how to surf just yet. Their parents can do that when they're ready. Some of my daughters still surf regularly, but I'm not sure Sloane has done much of it since having her boys.

"Papa, you should've brought your board," Josh calls out, getting my attention.

"Next time, buddy. I'm good jogging beside you for now. Are you two about ready to head home for dinner?"

"Not yet," Josh blurts, picking up speed again and darting forward, leaving us in the dust.

"Can we make s'mores?" Jason asks eagerly.

"If you eat a good dinner, I might be able to make that happen," I hedge.

I learned long ago never to promise anything I can't deliver.

Fortunately for them, I always keep a stash of marshmallows, chocolate, and graham crackers on the top shelf in the pantry for special occasions like this. It's well out of sight and is something I love surprising them with. Between that and blueberries in the freezer for pancakes in the morning, I'm always prepared for almost anything they throw at me. If not, I make sure I have it the next time they visit.

After missing so much of their childhood while being in the Air Force, I've made it my mission to make up for lost time. My mom was the best grandparent imaginable, and I'm doing my best to live up to the high bar she's set.

I'll never forget the day she punched her hands into her hips and told me in no uncertain terms, *"It's a grandparent's prerogative to have special traditions with my grandbabies."*

Since I consider her to be the top role model when it comes to grandparenting multiple grandkids, I've made making memories like longboarding and s'mores something every one of my grandkids can count on when it comes to *this* papa.

*I wonder what Faye would think of them.*

She adored kids when we were younger. Does she still feel the same?

Obviously, we didn't spend much time getting into deep conversation last night, but now that I'm away from her, I'm curious about her story.

*How on earth is she single and here in Seaside of all places?*

Beyond work, I'm dying to know what she's been up to for the past thirty years.

Sure, with a few swipes of my fingers, I could find out most of this on my own, thanks to my contacts with Riggs, but my gut tells me it's best to hear the full story from Faye, rather than do a deep dive into her private life.

As twitchy as I am to fill the gaps, she needs to tell me in her own due time.

"Papa!" Jason calls out, forcing me to stop thinking about Faye for the millionth time since parting this morning.

"What's up, Jay?" I ask as I purposely dart my eyes around him in search of any potential danger. It's unusual for him to shout in this tone at me.

Without missing a beat as he zips down the sidewalk, he rubs his stomach for emphasis and hollers, "I'm hungry."

Waiting until we safely pass the young family out for a summer evening stroll, I call out so Josh can hear. "Let's turn around. It's time to head home."

Once I'm sure Josh has slowed and is heading this way, Jason and I stop to wait for him. Then, as soon as they're both pointed in the right direction, I quickly drop a challenge I know they won't refuse. "Who wants to race home and get dinner started?"

"Can we help cook?" Josh asks with such eagerness there's no way I'd refuse his request.

"Of course. How else will you do it for yourself someday?"

"Papa," Josh adorably huffs in exasperation. "I'm five. Momma says we can't cook without a grown-up."

Shit, he's got me there.

Smacking my forehead as if that thought never crossed my mind, I grin and exaggeratedly shake my head. "She's right, you *do* need a grown-up, but there are plenty of things you can do to help with dinner. By the time you get to be my age, you'll be cooking with ease."

"Can we make smashed potatoes?" Jason asks eagerly.

This right here is why kids should name everything. I know I should correct him, but he's simply too adorable to contradict the words coming out of his mouth.

"Only if you help wash and peel them," I counter, knowing full well the two of these guys will somehow find a way to make it a competition.

"Do you have cob corn?" Josh asks. "Momma made some last night. It was yummy!" Christ, the way he's rubbing his stomach... There's no way I can say no to that, either.

"I'll tell you what. When we get home, we'll hop in my truck and head to the store. Then we'll come back and cook."

"Let's do it!" Josh shouts. Then, on his next breath, he adds, "I'll race ya home, Jay!"

"Ready... Set... Go!" Jason shouts, and the two of them pump like crazy, pushing their boards to the limit. I have no choice but to sprint after them and do my best to ensure they stay out of trouble.

---

MY HEART ZINGS when I turn onto my street and spot Faye outside, checking her mailbox.

How we didn't run into one another before this week is beyond me.

I can't help the smile that forms as I watch her long blonde hair flow in the light breeze. It's hard not to notice her curves on full display in dark, well-fitted jeans and a loose tank as she bends to check inside the box.

Damn, she's gorgeous.

With her back to me, memories from last night flood through me, and I revel in this small moment, since she doesn't immediately clock my approach.

As I roll down my window and pull up beside her, the boys take notice.

"Who's that, Papa?" Jason asks with interest.

When Faye's eyes meet mine, a wide smile spreads across her beautiful features. "Hey there." She chortles. "Fancy seeing you so soon, Mark." Then she glances from me to my grandsons. "Who do we have here?"

"Papa," Josh whisper-shouts, much louder than necessary. "Who is she?"

*Yeah, he's as subtle as a bull in a china shop.*

Amused by their curiosity, I turn and face the boys sitting in the back of my crew cab in their booster seats. "Boys, this is Faye. She lives next door." I point to her house because I'm sure that'll fly out of their mouths next. "Faye, these are Sloane and Jax's twins, Jason and Josh."

"What have you all been up to?"

"Papa took us longboarding," Josh chimes in.

At the same time, Jason says, "We went shoppin' for smashed potatoes and corn cobs." Then he puffs out his chest with pride and adds, "We're making dinner."

"Is that right?" Faye's amused expression melts my heart. "I hope your papa feeds you more than potatoes and corn on the cob."

"Of course," I jump in, patting the steering wheel for good measure, wishing my hands could reach out and push that wispy runaway lock of hair behind her ear. "We're having steak and mushrooms to go with our other vegetables." With a hopeful glance in her direction, I quickly add, "Care to join us?"

"And s'mores for dessert," Josh enthusiastically interjects. "Papa makes them."

"Oh," Faye draws out happily. "I haven't had s'mores in years. Those sound delicious."

I turn just in time to see Jason's mouth drop open. "Years? That's a long time. Papa makes the bestest ones."

Her knowing glance my way reminds me so much of when we were kids. "I remember that. Did you know your papa and I used to go to school together?"

"Really?" flies out of both boys' mouths at the same time.

But it's Josh who shares, "We're goin' to school this year, too!"

"That's right," I acknowledge. "You'll start kindergarten at the same school as your cousins and where Aunt Liz works."

"But not Everett, Embry, and Candace. They're too little," Jason interjects.

"They'll be there in due time," I counter.

"You've already got them longboarding, and they're not even in kindergarten?" Faye asks in disbelief.

"Uh... He taught us *last year*. We go real fast now!" I don't even have to look to know Jason's punched his hip and is cocking his head in challenge.

As a five-year-old, he thinks the world should already know his every move. Though that's likely because the adults around him can spot his plotting from a mile away.

This earns an amused chortle from Faye. "I don't doubt that. Your papa always loved longboarding."

"If I recall," I quickly add, raising a brow, "you weren't so bad at it either."

Faye shakes her head. "Oh, Lancaster. That ship has sailed."

"I'm sure if you gave it a try, it'd be like riding a bike."

"The risk isn't nearly worth the reward," she muses. "Besides, if I fell now, I'd likely break a hip or something."

"Sheesh, it's not like you're signing up for AARP or anything just yet," I tease.

"Ohmigoodness!" Faye quickly covers her mouth as she rolls her eyes in amusement. "I can't even with you, Lancaster."

Instead of pushing my luck further, I change tactics. "What do you say, Faye? Are you up for dinner with the boys and me? I've got plenty."

Faye tilts her head to the side, and an unreadable expression crosses her features. When she looks from me to the boys, I go for the jugular.

"How's that stomach of yours gonna handle my barbecue wafting through your windows if you stay next door? Besides, when was the last time you ate?"

Pulling a hand to her stomach, she rolls her lower lip under her teeth before sighing heavily. "My meeting went right through lunch, so... breakfast?"

"You need to eat," I pointedly remind her.

Crossing her arms over her chest, she grumbles. "I eat."

"I'll tell you what..." I counter. "Let's get you fed, then, if you're lucky, these boys and I will challenge you to a game of UNO. Fair warning, these two"—I turn their way to prove a point—"like to gang up on the unsuspecting."

Her beautiful laugh is music to my ears. "Who can refuse an offer like that? Just let me put my mail inside, and I'll be over —on one condition..."

"What's that?" Josh asks, fully invested in our conversation.

"That you let me help."

# Chapter 12
## Faye

My cheeks hurt from laughing as I drop down a *wild draw four* card onto the stack of UNO cards in the center of the table. I hesitate for a moment as I look my hand over, then quickly add, "I choose red."

"You've got to be kiddin' me!" Mark winces as he picks up another four cards and adds them to the collection he's acquiring in his hand. "The three of you must be ganging up on me."

"Do you need a card holder like us, Papa? I can help you look for one," Josh asks without an ounce of malice or sarcasm.

*Oh, my heart! These boys are the sweetest.*

I've always loved being around kids and consider myself to be an amazing aunt to my nieces and nephews. It doesn't hit often, but at times like this, I can't help but wonder what it would have been like if I'd had some of my own. Maybe if I hadn't been so focused on my career, things would've been different.

*Then again, that ship sailed years ago,* I quickly remind myself.

"I'm doing just fine, kiddo. But thanks," Mark snarks playfully, effectively drawing me out of my thoughts as he organizes the cards into his growing pile.

The boys each have their own card holder so they can keep track of their cards, with their hands being so tiny. I'd never even heard of such a thing, but when Mark pulled them out with the deck of UNO cards, I was impressed. If only something like this had been around when I was growing up. There's no way either of the boys could hold as many cards as Mark has in his hands.

Jason lays down a red three and shouts, "UNO!"

"Are you kiddin' me?" Mark protests. "I swear, you two are using your twin powers to beat me tonight. Just look at all these cards!"

The boys give each other a knowing look and beam with pride.

Looking at my three cards, I secretly hope Josh keeps the color as red so I can unload at least one more of them before this game is over.

When he places a red seven, I let out the breath I didn't know I'd been holding and place the red *Skip* card down, then glance to see Mark's reaction.

He doesn't disappoint.

"Looks like they're not the only ones out to get me," Mark grumbles, but when his eyes meet mine, they're full of mirth.

This earns him more hoots and hollers from the rest of us. Once the boys start laughing, it's infectious—hence my sore cheeks.

He warned me when we started that they play cutthroat, so no going easy on the boys—and he meant it. I've done my best to bring my A game. For a while, I thought Mark would pull off the win, but then I kept drawing *Draw Fours,* and when Josh reversed the playing order, Mark's been blessed with every last one of them.

I'd almost feel sorry for him *if* he hadn't dumped them on me to begin with.

Karma is real, and to my utter delight, Mark's feeling it about now.

When Jason draws, because he's apparently out of red, we all breathe a sigh of relief, and the playing continues.

When it's my turn, I'm forced to draw, as well.

"*If* this game ever ends," Mark emphasizes as he finally gets to play a card, "are you ready for s'mores?"

"Yes!" Jason and Josh both shout excitedly at once.

"After you each get *one*, if you come in and take a bath, I'll let you watch a movie before bed."

"Can we watch *Cars*?" Jason looks wide-eyed at Josh, who nods fervently.

"As long as you don't flood my bathroom first," Mark chortles.

Both boys shake their heads profusely.

But Josh suggests, "Maybe if we take a shower, we can watch more of the movie. Momma makes us shower when we're in a hurry."

Mark catches my eye and grimaces. "Always the negotiator, this one." But instead of answering the question, he says, "Let's focus on finishing this game so we can get to those s'mores."

Before I know it, Josh lays down the last card, and the game ends.

As Mark gathers the cards, I place my hand on his and offer, "Let me. Go start the fire. My sweet tooth is aching, and I've heard you make some of the best s'mores."

"You shouldn't eat sweets if your tooth aches," Jason advises, his voice filled with concern.

"Oh, I'm so sorry." I gasp at my mistake. I should have

known better. Of course, he'd take it literally. "That's not what I meant. I was just teasing your papa. He knows I've always had a weakness for anything chocolate."

When Jason eyes me speculatively, Mark jumps to my defense. "Yeah, buddy, it's a figure of speech. Her teeth are just fine, I'm sure."

My heart sputters when Mark reaches under the table to squeeze my leg in assurance, before he adds, "Who wants to help gather the kindling?"

That's all it takes for both boys to shoot out of their seats and head for the mudroom where they've left their shoes. The second we're alone, Mark leans in and brushes a quick kiss on my lips, leaving me breathless.

"Been dying to do that since the mailbox," he whispers.

"Papa, you ready?" one of the boys shouts from the other room.

If I had to guess, I'd bet it was Josh by the tone, but I can't be sure.

"Can we go outside?" the other one asks.

"Yes, but stay inside the yard," Mark warns. "I'll be right out."

Leaning in to rest his forehead against mine, he whispers, "Thank you so much for being here tonight."

"Why are you thanking me? I've been fed and am having the best time. It should be *me* who's thanking *you*."

"The kids will be in bed within the hour or two, tops. Wanna watch a movie of our own after they fall asleep?"

"I could be persuaded, especially if you feed me chocolate and keep looking at me like that."

"Oh, if they weren't here, I'd be having *you* for dessert instead, Faye."

Before I can respond, the back door flings open and, "Papa, we're ready!" fills the room.

"Be right out." With a wink, he adds, "I'm grabbing the sweets now."

Without another word, he stands from the table, walks to the pantry, and grabs something from the very top shelf. Returning, he reaches for my hand and whispers so only I can hear, "Since I can't feast on you again tonight, you ready for your consolation prize, sweetheart?"

Heat floods through me, and my need for this man grows beyond measure.

# Chapter 13
## Mark

Sloane may say showers are quicker, but I know better than to leave two five-year-old boys unattended for long. After ensuring their hair was properly washed, I left them for less than five minutes to finish up and make sure their pajamas and towels were ready.

I should've known better.

Not only do I return to a room full of giggles, but an arc of water manages to come over the top of the curtain and land directly dead center on my chest the moment I return.

*How the hell are they doing that?*

"Hey now!" my voice booms, and I hear a scurry from the other side of the curtain. "Water is supposed to stay inside the tub."

"Sorry, Papa," Jason calls out. "I didn't know my hands could bend water like that."

*Like what, exactly,* almost comes out of my mouth; however, I hold back, not wanting to encourage it further.

I should be upset, but even I can admit this newfound talent is slightly impressive.

Besides, it's only water, and my shirt took the brunt of it, and other than a little puddle on the floor, no harm was done.

Letting them know playtime is over, I remind them, "If you want to watch the movie, you need to get moving."

I hear the water turn off, and I hand them their towels. Once they're dried off and dressed in their pajamas, I send them out to Faye so I can make quick work of cleaning up the bathroom. Needing out of my now-soaked shirt, I quickly pull it over my head and add it to the pile of clothes I'll drop off at the laundry room before starting the movie.

As I hastily exit the bathroom to catch up with the boys, I practically plow into Faye.

When her hands land on my chest, she quickly spits out, "Oh, I'm so sorry," as I reach to steady her.

"Uh, why are you apologizing?" I chuckle as I track her darting her eyes in all directions but mine.

"I... Uh..." she starts, then cocks her head to the side, and as her beautiful smile takes my breath away, I almost don't hear her whisper, "What happened to your shirt?"

"Apparently, one of the boys discovered they had water-bending capabilities."

Her eyes go wide as saucers, and she gasps, "You're kidding," in disbelief.

Chuckling at her response, I shake my head at the memory. "I'm not even shocked at this point. When I walked in, some-how, there was a steady stream flowing over the shower rod that hit me square in the chest. I truly have no idea how they managed an arc like that... And frankly, I'm afraid to find out. God forbid, I encourage them to practice their new talents. Sloane will have my ass."

"Ohmigod, I can't imagine." Faye stifles another round of laughter.

"Did you need something?" I ask, realizing she's in the hallway for a reason.

"Just going to use the restroom before the movie. The boys said they pulled blankets from the guest room and are getting settled to watch the movie."

Looking toward the living room, it suddenly feels too quiet. "I'd better make sure that's all they're doing."

"You do that. I'll be out in a minute." Faye reaches up on her toes and pecks a kiss on my cheek. When she pulls back, I feel the warmth from her touch long after she slips into the bathroom and shuts the door in my face.

*How can she still have this effect on me after all these years?*

When a low thud from the living room draws my attention, I make haste to ensure nothing—or *anyone* with the luck of those two—is broken.

Thankfully, it's only Josh dropping blankets onto the floor. I watch him contemplate whether to lie on the floor or sprawl out on the soft cushions in front of him. Without a word, he quickly picks up his things and sets himself up on the couch.

Once he's settled, I spot Jason innocently crawling into my recliner. He and Josh have been taking turns sitting in my favorite chair since they arrived. Truthfully, if I need rack time, I'll sleep on a pile of rocks, but it makes them feel special, so I let them think what they will about the chair.

That leaves the loveseat for Faye and me.

*Ha. Who needs wingmen when I've got these two?*

"Can we have popcorn, Papa?" Josh asks.

"You got a hollow leg or something? Where are you putting all this food?"

He looks just like his mom when he drops his chin and slowly shakes his head at me. "There's always room for popcorn with movies."

"Are you sure about that?" I counter.

"Yeah, Papa," Jason pipes in. "We've got room."

"Hmmmm..." I draw out, contemplating my choices.

It's already been over an hour since we've eaten s'mores. They played soccer in the yard before coming in for their shower.

Fuck it. It's not gonna hurt them.

"Let me put these towels in the laundry and grab a shirt. Then I'll see about getting us popcorn."

By the time I slip my shirt over my head and return to the kitchen to make popcorn, Faye has joined the boys in the living room.

When she hears me open the pantry and pull out the air popper, she asks, "What are you making now?"

"Popcorn," the boys say in unison, and all I can do is smile.

I did this with my girls every chance I could when they were younger, too. As Mom would say, *I'm making memories*.

"Make yourself comfortable on the loveseat. I'll be right out." Just as I'm about to start the machine, a thought hits me. "There are plenty of blankets in the hall closet, if you wanna grab one for yourself."

To this day, my girls rarely watch movies without snuggling with a blanket. If I recall, Faye was the same when we were younger. Sometimes, I'd come home from work to find her and my mom snuggled on separate ends of our couch, watching some rom-com or another, especially after Mable went away to college.

Mom always did like Faye.

I shouldn't have been surprised they kept in touch. Faye spent just as much time at our house as she did at her own in high school.

*Wonder what Mom would think of us running into one another again.*

God, what I'd give to pick up my phone and tell her about this.

"Papa, is it ready?" Jason calls out the minute the kernels stop popping, and the room goes silent, bringing me back to the present.

"As soon as I pour on the melted butter and add some salt, I'll bring you each a bowl. Want some Faye?"

"Yes, please." Faye nods. "You sure you don't want help?"

"Start the show, and I'll dish everyone up. Want anything to drink while I'm at it?" I offer to the room.

Over the sound of the movie cueing up, I hear, "Milk, please," immediately followed by my other grandson shouting, "Me, too!"

"Faye? I've got soda, milk, water, and juice."

"One of those Pepsis I saw earlier would be great, thanks. You sure you don't need help?"

"I got it," I assure her as I set out bowls on the counter.

With popcorn and drinks passed out, I settle in beside Faye, just as the opening credits roll. She sighs heavily as she settles into the couch, and it takes everything in me not to wrap my arm around her and pull her close. With the boys mere feet away, I settle for stretching my legs out in front of me and resting my arm against hers between us.

The warmth of her skin and the scent of her perfume have every nerve ending in my body misfiring. I feel like I'm fighting a war with myself, forcing my limbs to remain in place.

*What is it about her that has me coming out of my skin?*

Maybe I haven't been around any woman in recent memory that I've wanted more with.

Being with Faye has always been as easy as breathing.

Maybe it's because we're older, but even after one night, this just feels different.

As I glance at each of my grandsons, I realize Faye's the first person I've ever considered bringing around my family. When I saw her this evening, it never even crossed my mind *not* to include her in our plans.

For as long as I can remember, I've kept women at bay because I knew I wouldn't have time for them or be able to put in the effort they deserved.

My girls came first—always. If I had leave, it was spent with them. Period.

Now that I'm retired, I'm doing what I can to make up for lost time with my family.

I'm jostled from my thoughts when Faye nudges me in the ribs and whispers so only I can hear, "You okay over there, Lancaster?"

"Uh... Just got lost in my head for a moment," I admit.

That's not a lie, but I'm not sure I'm ready to reveal my truth just yet.

I need to wrap my head around it first.

Hell, I'm not even sure where my line of thought is going.

*What does more even mean?*

Her brow quirks the way it used to when she was about to call me on my shit.

Just before she says what's clearly on her mind, I purposely dart my eyes toward my grandsons, hoping she'll get that now's not the time to have this discussion.

I watch her eyes narrow and lips purse, and I can see her indecision to let her instinctual worry go.

Needing to reassure her, I quickly reach for her hand, give it a squeeze, and hope it'll be enough to help her stop worrying. The moment my hand touches hers, her features relax, and I let go of the breath I wasn't aware I was holding.

Her implicit trust makes my chest squeeze.

Intertwining her fingers with mine, she nods once, then returns her attention to the movie as if she doesn't have a care in the world.

*If only life could stay this simple.*

# Chapter 14
## Faye

The last thing I expected was to fall asleep, but that's exactly what happened.

I blame Mark and the blanket he suggested I curl up with. Between the two of them and getting very little sleep the night before, it was the perfect trifecta to completely crash harder than I have in years.

I'm not even sure how long I've been asleep, but I'm certain it's been a while. My limbs feel like lead weights, and it takes everything in me not to fall back into my peaceful slumber as I listen to the steady beat of Mark's heart. His comforting arms hold me in place, and if I didn't have to go to the bathroom so bad, I'd stay wrapped around him like this for an eternity.

When I force myself to move, I feel him startle below me. "Everything okay?"

"Just need to pee," I admit groggily, as I pry my eyes open. When I spot light from the early morning sun filling the room, I bolt upright. "Holy shit. What time is it?"

"Zero five hundred," Mark says on a yawn.

"Mark," I whisper-shout. "How could you let me sleep like this?"

"Let you?" Mark laughs quietly. "I didn't *let* you do anything. You were out like a light just as fast as the boys were."

"You could've woken me." I push against his chest to get him to let go. "I should've gone home last night."

"Sweetheart, if it makes you feel any better, I fell asleep, too. Besides... I'll take this kink in my neck if it means waking up with you in my arms."

"Don't be ridiculous!" I swat playfully at his chest.

Pulling me back to lie against him, he whispers, "Maybe next time you stay over, we'll actually get good sleep."

"Now, what would be the fun in that?" I tease. "Are you turning into an old man on me?"

This earns me a playful eye roll as he shakes his head. "You may be the death of me yet."

"Hey now..." I hiss in warning.

"Just five more minutes," he pleads.

"Let me up to use the bathroom first, and I'll consider it."

He squeezes me quickly, then pats my hip. "Go. If we're lucky, the boys will be asleep for another hour or so."

By the time I return, Mark is nowhere to be found.

Not knowing what to do, I fold the blanket I used last night. *Maybe I should go?*

I'd hate for the boys to wake up and get the wrong impression.

Just as I place the blanket in the hall closet, I feel Mark's arms snake around my waist. "Uh... Where do you think you're going? I thought you said we'd snuggle some more."

Turning around, I wrap my arms around his neck. "You were gone, and well, it felt weird standing there. I'd hate for the boys to get the wrong impression."

"Hmmm..." he murmurs into my neck. "You smell good."

"Mark," I chastise. "What are you doing?"

"Wishing you a good morning." I hear the smile in his voice, even though I can't see it. "Will you stay for breakfast? I'm making blueberry pancakes... Are those still your favorite?"

"What will the boys think if they find me in the same clothes?" I point out.

Sighing heavily, he states, "They're five. I doubt they'll notice."

"Mark... they'll know. Even if they don't notice, you and I will."

"It's a good thing you live next door. Go home. Change, and I'll start cooking. Coffee will be ready by the time you return."

His offer sounds enticing.

As I mull over my schedule for the day, I admit, "I guess I don't have any pressing meetings until this afternoon."

"Good. Then it's settled. Even though I think you may be overthinking this, go home and change if it'll make you feel better. I'm just not ready for our time together to end."

"Mark, we're neighbors. It's not like I'm going that far."

"Not the point, sweetheart."

When his eyes lock onto mine, I know with every fiber of my being that he feels whatever this is going on between us as strongly as I do.

If I'm being honest, I'm not ready for my time with him today to end yet, either.

"All right." I sigh heavily. "Let me go home, shower, and change. Then, I'll be back for breakfast."

---

BY THE TIME I RETURN, Mark and the boys are bustling around the kitchen. He's put them to work, and they're cutting up bananas with butter knives, peeling mandarin oranges, and sneaking handfuls of blueberries when they think their papa's not looking. The smart man that he is bought two packages of blueberries as if he knew they'd be a hot commodity this morning.

"Look, Faye," Jason calls for my attention. "This blueberry is huge. You want it?"

"Oh, buddy." My heart squeezes at his thoughtfulness. When he shoves it in my direction, I have no other option but to say, "Thank you," and take it.

"Can you go swimmin' with us today?" Josh asks, handing me a slice of orange. "Here, eat this."

"Papa's taking us to our lesson," Jason chimes in. "We're going down the big slide today."

"Wow, that's really exciting! Are you doing them at the Astoria Aquatic Center?"

"Yeah, they're swimming at three," Mark states as he flips another pancake over, then bends to check on the bacon in the oven.

As Jason's long lashes bat in my direction, guilt crashes through me. "Unfortunately, I can't. I have meetings this afternoon."

Jason looks from me to Mark and back, then shakes his head and sighs heavily. "Papa's tired now. That's why he goes to our lessons."

*Tired? What's he talking about?*

Before I can fully clock what he's saying, Mark jumps in, "Yeah, Jay, I'm *retired*. That means I no longer work for the Air Force."

That sweet boy cocks his head to the side and narrows his brows. "But Momma said you worked last time."

"Yeah, that's why you didn't see us swim in the deep end," Josh chimes in.

"Well..." Mark plates the pancakes and turns off the griddle. "That's right. I was working. But now that I'm *retired*, I get to pick and choose when I work, so I can make time for our family."

*So, that's why he mysteriously disappeared for three days.*

I'd bet my last dollar it isn't just a random job either—no, this man is way too tight-lipped to have retired completely. Working in private security or other government agencies would be right up his alley.

*Don't think I don't notice you avoiding eye contact with me, either, Mark Lancaster.*

When he finally glances my way, then back to his grandsons, I make the split-second decision to let it go—for now.

The next time we're alone, all bets are off.

Pulling the bacon that had been warming in the oven, Mark brings the food to us. "Who's ready for breakfast?"

"Not sure how much they'll eat, since they've been snacking on fruit more than chopping it," I muse, looking at the plate of fruit they've set out for us.

"These two are always hungry, Faye. I swear, they each have hollow legs because their stomachs surely can't be this big."

The boys rock in laughter as they each reach for a pancake. As soon as Mark gives them some bacon, he offers some to me, then sits beside me on a barstool.

"Fresh coffee, crispy bacon, and homemade pancakes? A girl could get used to this," I tease after taking my first bite. "Mmmm... This is delicious."

Mark shrugs as he dishes up his own plate. "You've got an open invitation. With my family being so close, I keep the fridge stocked and ready for unexpected visitors. With summer in full swing, I do my best to help my girls when I can."

Maybe I've got his situation all wrong, "You watch the kids most days?"

"Only when needed. These two have Becca, their regular sitter, during the weekdays, but she had a family emergency. When Jax isn't touring or in the studio, he has a lot more flexibility to be with the boys, and Sloane tries to keep regular work hours when she's in town."

"So, their dad is a musician?"

"Daddy and Uncle Finn are Ruby Frax." Josh grins with delight.

Ruby Frax? "What?" I draw out as the pieces slowly click together. "Your daughter is married to Jax Cartwright?"

When Mark nods, I muse to myself, "How did I not know that?"

"I guess it never came up," Mark says with a shrug.

Then I remember the headlines from a few summers ago. "Wait... Those were your daughters who caused all that commotion with their mistaken identity when the world found out Jax was engaged?"

A low chortle escapes as he nods his head. "Yeah, Raven and Sloane are often mistaken for one another until you get to know them. Much like these two rascals." He points mischievously at each of the boys.

"I only pretend I'm him sometimes." Josh giggles guiltily.

"Oh, boy, that's not good." I can only imagine the trouble these two will get into when they're older.

"Wait, that must mean you're also related to Finn McGowen?"

"Yep, he's our uncle." Jason nods. "He's teachin' me the drums."

"What about you, Josh? Are you learning an instrument?"

Sighing, he shakes his head. "Daddy says we both need to

learn piano first. When our fingers are bigger, we can learn guitar."

"Hmmm... Your dad must know what he's talking about," I muse. "He's pretty good at what he does. I caught his concert when I was in London last year."

Mark's eyes go wide. "You watched them perform in London?"

"Yeah, I snagged some tickets at the last minute. I'd been wanting to see them when they performed here, but the timing never worked out."

"We were at that concert." Mark motions to all three of them. "Hmmmm... Talk about two ships passing in the night."

*What are the odds?*

Mark continues as if he didn't just drop a bomb on me. "We were in one of the VIP suites to keep our rowdy crew contained."

"I was up in the nosebleed sections. It was so last-minute, I took what I could get. Something just told me I needed to attend, so I went."

"Hmmm... Interesting," Mark muses as his eyes lock on mine. "Did you go with anyone?"

"Nope. I was there on business, and an ad popped up on my feed. As someone who travels alone frequently, it didn't even phase me to go solo."

"You can come with us next time," Jason offers.

Oh, this sweet boy will be stealing hearts for years to come with such thoughtfulness.

"I'll keep that in mind," I assure him. Then I remember Mark has two other girls, whom I know little about. "What about your other girls? I know one is married to the Murdock boy; what about the other?"

"Lanie, my oldest, is married to Ryan. I told you how they met, thanks to Mom. She's settled here in Seaside and teaches

English at the high school. Lizzy, my youngest, teaches elementary in town. She's married to one of the label execs, Cameron Kruse."

"Interesting... Did they meet through Ruby Frax?"

"Technically..." he draws out and squints one eye, "they met while she was in college at Portland State. Somehow, they both landed in Seaside that summer, and she ended up being Milli's nanny."

"Milli?" I haven't heard that name yet.

"She's our cousin," Josh boasts. "She's a good swimmer. She can hold her breath for a *long* time."

"Is that right?" I ask, completely amused by his excited expression.

"She may have her own pool to practice in, but if you keep working at it, you'll be just as good as her one day," Mark points out.

From the determined look in both boys' expressions, I can tell it's a challenge they both plan to meet.

Once we finish eating, I help clean up. Mark settles the boys into watching a show about learning letters, then comes to help with the dishes.

"I need to go home and get a few things done before my meeting."

Glancing at the boys, he says, "I'll be right back."

They're so engrossed in their show, they barely acknowledge Mark's words. Then he turns to me. "I'll walk you out."

As soon as we're out of sight of the twins, Mark reaches for my hand. "Thanks for coming back over. I hope it wasn't too chaotic."

"Are you kidding? I had the best time."

"Does that mean you'll do it again?"

Waking up in his arms certainly wasn't a hardship.

Regretfully, I sigh. "I've got a conference call at five a.m.

tomorrow morning. I need to bring my A game, so no late night for me today."

Opening the door so I can step onto the porch, he adds, "I'm not sure when Jax will return, but you're welcome for dinner again tonight. I promise I'll send you home in plenty of time to get a good night's rest."

As soon as the door shuts behind us, his arm wraps around my hip, and he pulls me close.

Inhaling deeply, I get lost in his masculine scent and rest my head against his chest. "Can I let you know when I'm done with work for the day? Depending on my call this afternoon, I could be sailing on easy street, or shit's gone sideways in a nanosecond. I won't know until I talk with my client and fully analyze the modifications and specs I created yesterday."

Brushing his fingertips along my jaw, he guides me to meet his gaze. "If you have to work... I, of all people, get it. Please know the invitation is out there, and I'd love for you to join us."

Leaning down, he brushes his lips against mine.

It starts out as an innocent kiss, but the moment I open my mouth to his, a tsunami of heat flows between us. One of Mark's hands snakes into my hair and tilts my head in just the right angle that I'm completely consumed by him.

Every nip, suck, and stroke of his tongue makes me crave him more.

God, how I wish I could stay wrapped in his arms until the end of eternity.

There's something about being with him that has me wishing for things I haven't thought of in years. He makes me wish for more, and I'm not ready to think about how I feel as a result.

Nope, I just want to stay in the here and now and not waste the gift of our paths crossing again.

When a car horn blasts from a distance, I'm brought back to

reality, making my brain register—*we're in public.* His grand-kids are just on the other side of that door, and the last thing either of us needs is for them to seek him out and catch us making out like randy teenagers.

Mark must feel the moment my brain returns to the reality we're living in because he, too, slows our kiss and eventually breaks it.

The heat in his eyes could make a smart woman like me do very stupid things.

"I-I gotta get going...." I sputter regretfully.

"Can I see you again later?" Mark asks, slowly wiping his thumb over my swollen lips.

"I'll let you know when I'm done with my calls," I whisper, wishing I could give him a definitive answer.

"Okay, sweetheart, you do that."

Pushing me back, he grips my shoulders and turns me toward my house.

"Go... Kick ass and conquer the world. I'll be here waiting when you're done!"

# Chapter 15
## Sisters Group Chat

LANIE:

Do we expect any less from Sloane? (rolling eyes emoji)

SLOANE:

Yeesh... some of us have to work year-round and don't have summers off.... ANYWAYS... I found two amazing bands I'm trying to sign.... (head exploding emoji)

LIZZY:

If anyone can close those deals, it's you. (dragon slayer sticker)

RAVEN:

Have your boys broken Dad yet? I haven't heard from them today.

SLOANE:

Ha ha... he's fine... or at least he hasn't said otherwise. (shrugging emoji)

LIZZY:

I ran into them long boarding this afternoon. They all look to be in one piece.

SLOANE:

God. I miss them like crazy... Jax, too. Why is NYC so far away? (sad face emoji)

LANIE:

I can't imagine. But you'll be home as soon as you can, AND you'll bring two new acts with you! (champagne emoji)

SLOANE:

From your lips to God's ears, as Nana would say.

SLOANE:

Oh, since we're all here... you'll never guess what I heard today!?!?!

RAVEN:

That turkey sandwiches do taste better with Doritos on them?

LANIE:

What is wrong with you?

RAVEN:

Apparently, my kids are the only ones with superior taste buds as they insisted I make sandwiches like that today. I blame Milli. She's the one who showed them.

LIZZY:

She's not wrong. (Shrugging emoji)

SLONE:

HELLO! I'm trying to talk here... Anyways... Word on the street is that Dad invited the neighbor over to watch movies and eat s'mores last night.

RAVEN:

Mrs. Rimer must have kept her hearing aids on low and just enjoyed the sweet treats.

SLOANE:

The boys couldn't stop talking about Dad's neighbor. Apparently, they played UNO and watched a movie together, and she even came over for breakfast this morning.

LANIE:

When your boys aren't trying to dominate the world, they really can be sweet. I'm glad they included her. You know her kids hardly ever come around.

LIZZY:

So Dad just invited her over? Or did she invite herself?

SLOANE:

I don't know… but however it happened, the boys were on cloud nine. They wouldn't let me get a word in edgewise.

LANIE:

That is really sweet. I've seen her watching the kids while they play in the yard. Maybe we should invite her over for family dinners.

RAVEN:

She may like the Lancasters better in small doses. We're A LOT when we're together. I'd be happy to invite her next time I see her, though.

LIZZY:

Gotta run. We're heading to story hour. Will we see any of you there?

SLOANE:

Not me. (crying emoji)

RAVEN:

Girls are still at camp.

LANIE:

I'm in. See you in twenty.

SLOANE:

Give my boys a hug for me if you see them. I hope I wrap this up soon.

# Chapter 16
## Mark

Just as I'm pulling our pot roast for dinner out of the InstaPot, my wrist buzzes with an incoming text.

HARPER:

Got a minute?

With Enzo Harper, it could be several things, so I set my roast on the plate I have set out, then pull my phone out of my pocket and call him. He picks up right away.

"Hey, man. What's up?" I ask in greeting.

"Hey, Mark. I've got a situation."

Shit. This can't be good. "Okay..."

"I've promised my wife I'd accompany her to a big book event in Germany this week, and Carson's celebrating his anniversary in Belize. Any chance I can talk you into doing a quick transport to DC? You'd be on standby while Riggs meets with the brass. If all goes well, it would be a two-day trip, tops. I know you're trying to stick around home this summer, but I'd owe you big time if you could step in for me."

Glancing at my grandsons playing Legos in the living room,

I ask, "How soon is wheels up? I'm on kid detail until Jax returns from LA."

If I can help Enzo, I will. He rarely calls in personal favors.

"We're still waiting on the green light, but the goal is to leave tomorrow night or the next morning and return within twenty-four hours."

"When I spoke with Sloane earlier, she said Jax and the guys are hoping to catch a flight home this evening...." I draw out, working out the details in my head. When I don't see any major obstacles, I concede. "I should be able to make this work."

"Thanks, man. You're a lifesaver! Not only will Riggs be happy, but I'll score major points with my wife. Germany is a special place to us, and it's rare when we get away without our littles in tow. Between you and my parents, I'll be indebted for a long time to come."

"I remember those days." I laugh, thinking about what it was like when my girls were younger. There's never a dull moment.

Enzo has ten-year-old twins, as well as three older bonus kids, as he calls them. The stories he tells about each of them, but especially Loren and Raine, are wild, to say the least. While I get to send my chaotic brood home, Enzo's still in the thick of things.

"Riggs says you're flying solo with your grandsons this week. Are they givin' you a run for your money?"

"You could say that. But we're making do." I chuckle, then admit, "Truth be told, I wouldn't trade this time with them for the world. They certainly keep me on my toes, but we're having the best time, ya know? You should've seen them on their longboards this afternoon... Man, they were crushing it."

"Oh, boy. I can only imagine the trouble the three of you can get yourselves into."

"The key is to keep them busy, my friend... Keep them so busy they crash early and sleep hard as a rock."

Enzo's chuckle is infectious. "That only works when you're with them for short bursts. Sam and I are already busy enough as it is. You have the benefit of sending them home once you've tired them out. Cranky kids are no fun. Ever. Trust me."

"Being a grandparent is the best!" I muse. "Just wait and see...."

"Oh, my wait won't be long, my friend. We just got word Maddie and her husband are expecting their first this Thanksgiving."

"Congratulations, Papa! That's exciting!"

"We're in for one hell of a treat this holiday season."

"That you are. Enjoy every moment of it."

"Papa, I'm thirsty," Josh interrupts from the living room.

Before I can respond, Enzo interjects, "Listen, I'll let you go. We'll catch up when I return. The kids have been asking to visit the coast this summer. Maybe we can meet up."

"Anytime, Harps," I offer, reaching into the cupboard for some cups. "Just let me know when you're coming, and I'll fire up the grill."

"Roger that, and thanks again. Riggs will be in touch."

"I'm sure he will. Say hello to Sam for me, and enjoy your trip."

"Will do," Harper says before disconnecting the line.

"Who's ready for dinner?" I holler to the room. "Josh, I've got milk or apple juice. What will it be?"

"Juice," both boys say in unison, and they jump up from their projects on the floor.

Just as we're dished up, there's a knock at the door.

Instantly, I wonder if it's Faye, but before I can move, it swings open.

Disappointment rushes in when I register that she wouldn't

be comfortable enough to just walk in. But then I hear a loud, masculine voice call out, "Man, this place smells amazing," and my heart picks up a beat.

*Maybe there's hope to spending time with her this evening after all.*

Jax's booming voice fills the room as he walks into sight. "Did I make it just in time for dinner?"

"Daddy!" the boys shout excitedly, as they dash across the room to greet him. Both boys throw themselves at him with a force that could knock over a grown man if they're not prepared. In a well-practiced move, he bends in one fluid motion and scoops the two of them into his arms, where he hugs them tight. "God, I've missed you."

As soon as they squirm, he sets them down, and they rush back to their plates.

"Have you eaten? There's plenty to go around."

Jax rubs at his stomach. "I haven't. Mmmm... I wasn't hungry until I walked in."

Before sitting down, he grabs himself a plate from the cupboard and a glass of milk.

"How was your trip?" I ask once he's settled.

"Honestly..." he draws out, then hesitates. He cocks his head to the side and scratches at his chin. "Somehow, a total disaster of a trip turned into the most unexpected blessing we could've hoped for."

"What do you mean?" I ask, curiosity piqued.

"At first, the guys and I were pissed that we were stuck in LA due to the storm. We were told this would be a quick trip, and our families would hardly know we were missing. But the unexpected storm forced a production delay, as you well know."

I nod, wondering where he's going with this. Sloane never mentioned anything positive happening, other than the shoot finishing. Though, from Jax's animated expression and the way he's fighting back a grin, something tells me whatever his news is, it's big.

"Well... Long story short, the guys and I were dinking around. Just messing with a few chords and lyrics, and a movie producer heard us. He told us how much he liked the sound and flippantly wondered if we could write a song worthy of his next project. The film is wrapped, but the music score is off, so he's been stuck searching for the right sound. He spent a few minutes explaining the plot and conflict of the movie, and I kid you not, we wrote the perfect song for him in less than twenty-five minutes."

"Seriously?" I gasp in disbelief.

I know the guys have talent, but that's fast, even for them.

"You know Charlotte Ann, that romance author who's married to Luke Leighton, the coach of the Renegades?"

"Yeah." I'd have to be living under a rock to not know those two. "The girls read her books, I'm sure of it."

"Exactly. I've even listened to some of her books on audio because Sloane loves her work. Anyways... Each book in her latest series is being adapted into full-length films, and the producer who heard us said our song would be perfect. He pitched it to the other producers, and just as we got into town, our manager says he received a contract for the use of our song."

"Congratulations! That's great news!"

"No, Mark... You don't understand. This series has a bigger fanbase than you'd imagine. The films are predicted to become a major hub of pop culture if the initial sales are anything to go by. The books flew off the shelves. There were major release parties for each book in the series across the country. These parties grew with each new release. The series made Charlotte Ann a household name... And thanks to being stuck in LA, our new song will be a part of the original sound-track. This has the potential to launch Ruby Frax into the next stratosphere."

"Holy sh—" I start, then realize I should hold my tongue in front of the twins. "That is incredible news. When will it release?"

"Near the holidays. We'll officially record the song in the studio next week, with some extended versions. Then we'll get it to the production company."

"Any word on when Sloane returns?"

"Not sure. When we talked a few hours ago, she said she's staying an extra day back east to catch a show in Boston tomor-row, but she's not entirely sure if it'll pan out."

Shit. I just made plans to be out of town.

"Is Becca back? Or will the two of you need more help? I, uh... Got called in for a quick trip to DC."

"I've got it covered," Jax assures me with a grin. "Between my parents and everyone else in town, I'm sure I can get someone to watch the boys for the few hours I'll be in the studio."

"Can I have more carrots?" Jason asks, holding up his plate.

"Please," Jax reminds him.

Jason briefly purses his lips, then quickly turns to me with a smile I can't refuse. "Papa, can I *please* have more carrots?"

Reaching for the spoon, as the dish is on the other side of me, I ask, "Want more than carrots?"

"Can I have that potato, too?" He points to a small yellow one in the bowl. "Those were yummy."

"Me, too, please," Josh chimes in as he holds up his plate.

"After we clean up from dinner, Aunt Emily is in town and wants to see you."

"Aunt Emily! Do we get to see Grammy and Papa Cartwright, too?" Josh bursts with excitement.

"Yeah, can we see them?" Jason echoes with such joy, I can't help but grin.

"Of course! You know they love seeing you boys."

"Your family is always welcome here, Jax," I quickly remind him, then add, "If I'd known your sister was in town, I would've invited her over myself. I'm sure she'd love to see the boys."

"Oh, they know. Em just arrived today," Jax assures me. "I didn't even know she was coming until she called on her way out here." Jax shakes his head and shrugs. "Leave it to Emily to always keep us on our toes."

"With my four girls, that was always the case, trust me."

# Chapter 17
## Faye

I'm so engrossed in the code I'm working on that I barely register the knock at my door, until there's a second one. After saving my work, I stand from my desk. My body is stiff from hours of being in the same position. Flexing my fingers, I roll my neck from side to side, my muscles protesting with each step I make toward the door.

I spot a tall shadow through the top glass, and I don't even need a peek to know who it is. It's Mark. I just know it. Without hesitation, I swing it open.

The moment our eyes lock, a slow, sexy grin spreads across his handsome features, as he blatantly looks me over from head to toe.

I'm sure I'm a hot mess. My hair is barely contained in a top knot, I've put on an old cozy burnt-orange cardigan, and I'm wearing my large blue light glasses to take away some of the glare from my computer screens. My eyes are so dry, I'm blinking like crazy to bring some moisture back.

"Hey, sweetheart. Hope I'm not interrupting."

"No," I say on a yawn, stretching my body fully. "I'm at a good stopping place for the day."

"Have you eaten?" Mark asks, cocking his head to the side to study me.

"Not since..." I glance at my watch. "Shit... Breakfast, I think?"

Brow raised, he asks, "Do you make a habit of skipping meals?"

"Only when I get locked into a project," I admit. Which is way more often than I'll ever concede to him. When I'm on a roll, nothing gets in my way.

"Do you like pot roast, potatoes, and carrots?"

"I like anything I don't have to cook," I admit, suddenly ravenous for anything I can get my hands on. I'd thought about making something earlier, but obviously, I got sidetracked.

"Well, you're in luck. I brought you something for dinner," he says, handing me a container of food I didn't realize he'd been holding.

"I don't know what I've done to deserve you," I mutter, reaching for the dish.

"The bar is fairly low if you're impressed with leftovers," Mark deadpans. "Mind if I come in?"

"God, where are my manners? Of course. Wait..." I stop, glancing toward his house. "Where are the boys?"

Waggling his brows, he smirks. "At home..." He pauses dramatically, then adds, "With their dad. They left a few minutes ago. Since I haven't heard from you today, I hope you don't mind me dropping by unannounced."

My stomach rumbles when I take the top of the Tupperware container off and lay it on the kitchen counter. "You're always welcome, Lancaster. Especially if you come bearing gifts as delightful as this."

"Somebody's gotta make sure you're fed... Apparently." He

smirks, then a wicked grin quickly appears. "I'll happily volunteer as tribute if it means making you smile like that more often."

Leaning in, he quickly kisses me on the lips.

If I weren't suddenly starving for actual food, I'd consider getting lost in him for a while. When I pull back and glance at the steaming pot roast, he points to the tub. "Eat."

Since it's still warm, I do as I'm told. Pulling a fork from my drawer, I stab a piece of meat with it. It's so tender, it falls apart effortlessly. Popping it into my mouth, I moan in satisfaction. "Mmm... Mark. This is wonderful. Did you spend all day slow-roasting it? It's utter perfection."

"Nope..." He grins with delight. "I've got a magical pot that cooks it in minutes."

"What the hell are you talking about?"

"An InstaPot. Ever heard of it?" Mark waggles his brows adorably.

"Yes," I scoff, then admit after taking another bite. "But never knew it could cook a roast like this. I thought you could only get food to taste this savory from cooking it all day in a crockpot."

"My daughters gave me the gadget a few years ago, and it revolutionized my meal planning. Even though it's only me most nights, I still use it regularly."

"I never think that far in advance," I admit.

"Hey, perpetual bachelor here... I get that more than you'll ever know, trust me."

"You and I are on the same page, Lancaster. Though it's easier to get takeout than cook for one... Unless you're in this small town. Then, your options are quite limited."

"Seaside is much better than it was when we were kids." Mark shrugs as he brushes a piece of hair back from my face while I take another hearty bite.

"No kidding," I snicker. "There's something to be said about living in big cities. New York had every kind of takeout imaginable. God, I remember there was this one Italian restaurant right around the corner from my dorm that served six different kinds of homemade pasta, with twelve different kinds of sauce. It always hit the spot when I needed it most. I'd even make the trek from my apartment on the Upper West Side years after graduation, when I craved it."

"Do you still stop by if you're in the city?"

"When I can. Though if I'm there on business, I rarely have time."

"Speaking of business. There's something I feel I should tell you."

A tingle sprints up my spine, and I'm suddenly on full alert.

"What's that?" I ask hesitantly.

"So... Remember my three-day disappearance after running into you earlier this week?"

"Ha..." I practically snort. "How could I forget?"

"Your assumption was right... to a point. Although I've officially retired from the Air Force, I haven't fully clipped my wings."

"Okay..." I draw out, wondering where he's going with this.

"In the spirit of full disclosure—or at least to the point I'm allowed to share—you need to know that since I retired, I've been working for a private contractor."

"Good to know my instincts were correct." I smirk knowingly. "You tried to skate around it when I asked about it earlier. Guys like you just don't retire."

"No, I don't suppose we do...." he muses with an impish grin. "The point I'm failing to make is that I'm transporting my boss to DC. If all goes well, I'll be gone for less than two days."

"I assume you don't disclose this info freely?"

His expression turns stoic. "Nope. Mostly on a need-to-know basis."

Quirking a brow, I can't help myself. "And you think I need to know?"

"Yeah. I'm not about to disappear twice on you within a week. I may be out of practice, but I'm far from stupid."

"Out of practice?" What the hell is he talking about?

His lips quirk to the side, and his eyes never leave mine. "I made a vow to you years ago that I'd always give it to you straight."

"Wouldn't want it any other way," I admit, feeling my chest warm at his sincerity. "But what exactly are you out of practice from? It doesn't make sense. You fly regularly, I presume."

Drawing in a heavy breath, he reaches for my hand and squeezes it gently.

"Faye, aside from those few years I was married, I haven't been in a serious relationship with... well, anyone."

"Oh." That's certainly unexpected.

*But where's he going with this? Why this sudden change of tone?*

"What I'm saying is, you're important. We literally just reconnected days ago, and I don't want to push you away or have you thinking I'm not interested when I leave town again in such a short time."

"Okay..." I draw out, still unsure what to say in response.

This earns me an eye roll and a heavy sigh. When I don't say anything further, he continues. "I'm not sure where you are with *this* situation..." He slowly points between the two of us. "But I, for one, would like to see where it goes. I'm not trying to sound cocky or anything, but our connection is stronger than I ever could've imagined after all this time apart. I can't be the only one feeling this way... Am I?"

Thank God, I'm not going crazy.

I haven't wanted to put much stock into our intense connection. I've tried keeping things spontaneous and doing my best to just go with the flow. But this is Mark Lancaster; I should've known I'd never be able to accomplish casual. It's like every feeling I've ever had for this man has resurfaced without even being aware they existed in the first place.

I always thought it was just because Mark was my first love that I never felt such an intense connection like ours with anyone else. Hell, when I really clock my feelings, I spent nearly a decade with a man I was barely lukewarm with. Nothing has ever measured up since Mark and I broke up.

But after less than a week back in contact with Mark, I know without a doubt, it was simply *us*. No further explanation necessary. I have no idea what the hell this means, but I'm glad he doesn't want to see this end just yet either.

"Faye? You gonna say something?"

"Oh. Shit. I guess I didn't share my thoughts aloud...." I impishly snicker. Only Mark would have me so tongue-tied I'd forget to respond.

"Ha... Nope, you've left me twisting in the wind over here."

Reaching out my hand, I cup his face and assure him, "We're on the same page, Mark."

His features immediately relax, and for the longest moment, neither of us says anything. His perceptive hazel eyes stare deep into my soul. It's like he's reset time, and there's never been any distance between us.

Instantly, I've been transported to those carefree days when we were teens.

The logical side of me knows that's impossible. There's obviously so much I still don't know about him. The last few days have been such a whirlwind, I'm not even sure which side is up when it comes to Mark Lancaster.

Squeezing my free hand, he regains my attention. "What's

going on in that head of yours? I can tell your wheels are spinning again."

"How is it, despite our years apart, being with you is as easy as breathing?"

"Ha... Ain't that the truth." He exhales deeply. "I'm not sure what's going on, but I haven't stopped thinking about you since I ran into you the other morning. I loved spending time with you and the boys last night." Leaning closer, his voice deepens, "Listen... I know you've got an early morning, but any chance I could talk you into hanging out tonight, if I promise to get you in bed at a decent time?"

"Depends on what you have in mind," I tease, pulling him in for a kiss.

There's nothing sweet or slow about this kiss.

No, it's primal, searing, and the kind of kiss that could make you forget your own name. I'm vaguely aware of him pulling me closer. Then he lifts me and sets me on the counter of the island in front of him. When he steps between my thighs, I lock my heels around his waist and hold on tight.

God, he feels amazing.

The heat from his body against mine makes me burn with desire.

Tugging at his shirt, my fingers itch to feel his skin against mine.

In one fluid motion, he breaks our kiss to remove his shirt. Then, his gaze nearly incinerates me as he watches me quickly tug off my cardigan and rip my T-shirt over my head.

When I'm left in only my lacy bra, he wraps his arms around me and closes the distance between us. Burying his face in my neck, the hairs on his muscular chest tickle my skin. After squeezing me tight, he trails hot kisses along my collarbone and down my chest.

"God, you taste incredible. I can't get enough."

When he rolls my nipple with his thumb through the lace, a guttural moan I barely recognize as my own escapes.

"God, Mark... More."

Trailing hot kisses down my torso, my body pulses with desire.

With a firm hand, he presses my back against the cool granite.

I barely register the chill that races up my spine as his hands make quick work of unbuttoning my jeans and tugging them off.

Running his tongue along my hip, he moans, "Christ, Faye, you always wear the sexiest panties. Someday, I'll take the time to appreciate them, but I need to taste you more than I need my next breath."

Within seconds, he's got my panties past my ankles and has pulled me to the edge of the counter. His wicked grin captivates me as he murmurs, "Fuck, you're beautiful, sweetheart... But those sexy thighs will look even better wrapped around my shoulders."

"God, you're ridiculous." I laugh as he manhandles me to the place where he wants me.

"No, I'm efficient." His words are the last thing I register before that sensual tongue of his licks up my center.

"Fuuuuckkkk...." I moan, gripping the edge of the counter, needing something to keep me anchored to earth.

His warm breaths and quick strokes around my clit have me rolling down a runway, ready for takeoff. When two long fingers slip inside, he quickly finds a relentless rhythm, and before I know it, I'm teetering on the edge.

In and out, in and out. He keeps a steady pace, like he doesn't have a care in the world. When his tongue flicks my clit, my body tightens and electricity tingles deep in my spine.

"So close..." I pant out. "More... Mark. I need... more..." I beg.

Adding another digit, he presses deep and curls his fingers to massage my inner wall.

"Holy fuck... Right... There..." I fist my fingers into his hair and grind my pussy onto his face. The moment he sucks the nub of my clit into his mouth and flicks it with his tongue, I see fucking stars.

My entire body convulses, and it's all I can do to just ride wave after wave of this endless pleasure. When my tremors eventually still, I can't help but wonder, "What. The. Fuck. Did you just do to me?"

Pushing my thighs further apart to make room for his shoulders, he grins down from above me. "I can't be certain, but I think I just found my new favorite pastime. That was the sexiest thing I've ever experienced."

"You're ridiculous, Lancaster," I feign nonchalance, but truth be told, my body zings to life at his declaration.

That was freaking hot.

I may never look at this countertop the same way again.

Brushing loose strands from my face, he kisses me tenderly.

*Gah, this man knows just how to melt me from the inside out.*

When he pulls back, he says, "I truly did have plans to take you somewhere. Care to get dressed so I can steal you away?"

# Chapter 18
## Faye

Thirty minutes later, we're at the airfield, and he's going through the last of his pre-flight checks. I'm sitting beside him in a freaking cockpit of all places, and we're about to take off.

He still won't tell me where we're going, but he's assured me it won't be far.

As soon as we're cleared for takeoff, Mark does all the things necessary to get us safely down the short runway and into the air. My stomach dips as we climb higher and higher.

Until we're settled, I focus on the luscious green peaks of the hillside in the distance. Seeing it from the road is one thing, but up in the sky, where there are no obstructions, I fully grasp the vastness of these beautiful forests near Seaside.

"So, what do you think?" Mark asks once we've leveled off.

The sky is turning various shades of pink and orange as the sun begins to set. "I've never seen the coast from this perspective. It's incredible."

A wide grin spreads across Mark's features, and he nods. "I thought you might say that. Let's take a peek at the bridge in Astoria, then we'll head south along the coast for a bit."

"Everything looks so small," I whisper in wonderment.

"Oh, look, there's the elk." I point to a clearing just outside of town. "There must be close to a hundred of them bedding down in that field."

"I'm always in awe at just how many live outside our beaten paths."

"No kidding, though we see them at my parents' place from time to time."

"For some reason, my grandkids call them *fuzzy butts*." Mark chuckles. "Now, I can't ever see them and not want to do the same. Milli, my oldest, can spot them from miles away."

"That's adorable," I muse as the Astoria bridge comes into view.

The water from the Columbia River shimmers in the light as a large cargo ship passes under the highest part of the bridge.

"Wow..." I gasp. "The mountains are out." In the distance, I can spot both Mount St. Helens and Mount Adams behind it. Living on the other side of the coastal range, I often forget we're this close to the Cascades, too.

"You ready to head south? We can fly over our place and turn around after we check out Haystack Rock, if you'd like."

Within minutes, we're zipping along the coast. Everything appears small in comparison to us.

"Look here." Mark points to a neighborhood below. "That's where we live, and over here is where my girls live. Oh, damn, there they are. That's Lanie and Ryan with their kids out on the back deck of Mom's place. Carter is six, and Candace is five. She loves everything that's pony related, and he's a Lego fiend, much like Jason and Josh."

"It's too bad we can't let them know it's you."

"Next time." Mark nods in agreement, then points to the houses below. "Sloane and Jax live right next door on the right, and on this next block..." He points to a different location. "Raven and Finn live in that two-story house at the corner."

"Wow, your kids really do live close. Your mom would've loved that." His girls were Jane's pride and joy. It was evident every time I visited. Sighing heavily, I admit a truth I haven't said aloud in ages. "If I'd had kids of my own, I could only hope they'd be as close as your family is."

"I'm pretty lucky." Mark nods, then reaches for my hand and gives it a squeeze, as if he knows I need it. "Everything okay, Faye?"

"Yeah," I exhale slowly. "I'm good."

"Then what is it?" he presses, clearly sensing something is off.

I snort out a laugh at how unexpectedly things hit me at times. "It's funny, I spent my teens and early twenties taking every precaution and avoiding kids at all costs. I focused on school and always put my career first. Corey never wanted kids, and honestly, with him, I didn't either. We weren't a good fit. I'd never been more relieved than when I had my hysterectomy because I'd spent years bleeding way heavier than any human ever should. But seeing the joy your family brings you, I can't help but wonder, what if... You know?"

He squeezes my hand tighter. "I can't imagine what you might be feeling, but I can empathize. What-ifs are brutal."

"I do my best to live life without regrets," I assure him. "There's no point otherwise. I know with every fiber of my being that it truly was never the right time for me to have a family of my own. I wasn't in the right place or with the right person, for that matter."

For a few moments, a comfortable silence settles between us.

Eventually, Mark clears his throat and says, "Can I tell you something I haven't told many others? Did you know Sarah and

I got pregnant with Lanie just six weeks after meeting? Then we had four kids in three years, all while I was deployed twice during that time. I wouldn't trade my girls for anything, but I also wasn't the husband or father they always needed me to be. I had a phenomenal career in the Air Force, but that meant I had commitments where I couldn't always put my family first."

"I'm sure they understood," I assure him.

"It's why I work so hard to be as involved as I can now that I'm retired. I missed so many things while I was stationed around the world or deployed."

"What you did was admirable, Mark."

"But at what cost?" he ponders.

I assume it's a rhetorical question, as only he knows the answer.

Sighing heavily, he adds, "All we can do is the best we can, with the cards we're dealt. We can spend our entire lives on the could've, would've, or should'ves, but that won't do anything but make us miserable."

Taking in what he's saying, I sigh heavily. "I suppose you're right."

"Of course, I am. I'm always right." He grins and exaggeratedly puffs out his chest in pride. Then he pulls his hand from mine and puts it back on the steering mechanism to turn the aircraft around.

I'm lost in thought as we return to the airport. Within minutes, we've touched down, and he's doing his post-flight procedures. Or at least that's what I think it's called.

Once we've disembarked the plane and are back in Mark's truck, he throws me for another loop when he calls out my name. "Hey, Faye?"

"Yes, Mark? I repeat deliberately, matching his tone of voice.

"It's only seven-thirty. I'm nowhere near ready for our time together to end. Mind if we head to my place and watch that movie we never got to see? If you sleep over, I promise to wake you in time for your meeting in the morning."

"I think I could be persuaded, Lancaster."

Then I throw down a challenge of my own. "But... What do you say to skipping the movie and going straight to bed? Ever since you showed up and went down on me, I've been dying to get my hands and mouth around that cock of yours and have my way with you."

"That, sweetheart, is something I can *certainly* get on board with."

# Chapter 19
## Sisters Group Chat

RAVEN:

Okay, back up. What the hell are you talking about?

LIZZY:

Let's be clear… I didn't SEE anything… but I can't unhear it either. (Monkey covering ears emoji)

SLOANE:

What does this have to do with sweet old Mrs. Rimer?

LIZZY:

Sloane, you're the one who said he invited her over. I'm certain you're WRONG… unless Dad's into doing it with someone older than Nana.

RAVEN:

(head exploding emoji) What are you talking about?!?!?!

LIZZY:

Also… I'm fairly certain Mrs. Rimer's first name isn't Faye… so there's that.

SLOANE:

Who's Faye?

LIZZY:

I was out on a walk last night and saw Dad's garage door was open. So, I walked in through the mud room.

RAVEN:

And…

LIZZY:

Dad wasn't alone.

LANIE:

He's allowed to have a life. He may be our
dad, but he's not dead.

LIZZY:

Oh, Dad is far from dead, trust me. He was
having the time of his life.

RAVEN:

Wait... are you saying you walked in on Dad
having sex?!?!?!

LIZZY:

If he wasn't, he was about to...

LANIE:

OMG... that's hilarious!

RAVEN:

About as hilarious as him walking in on Finn
and me a few weeks ago. Serves him right.

SLOANE:

That's what you get for trying to have a
quickie in the garage when your kids are
watching TV upstairs. (eye roll emoji)

RAVEN:

Hey now... my husband's hot, and there's
only so much time in the day.

LIZZY:

How do you think I ended up with three kids?

SLOANE:

Twins are the reason my tubes are tied, and I
get all the hot sex I want!

LANIE:

I get it... y'all think your husbands are hot—as you should. Ryan's most certainly at the top of my list... But we were talking about DAD!!!! Focus, people...

SLOANE:

Are you sure that's what you heard? I've never seen or heard of Dad dating ANYONE!

LIZZY:

I'm still washing my ears out with bleach. I have a very active sex life... I know what it sounds like!

RAVEN:

You don't have to date to have sex. Before Finn, that was always my MO. Maybe Dad's taking a page out of my old book?

LANIE:

I know he's our dad, but I'm certain he hasn't been a monk all these years. Gah... do you remember how all our friends used to think he was so hot?

LIZZY:

Ewww... my friends never did that!

RAVEN:

Mine did. (shrug emoji)

SLOANE:

Same here.

LANIE:

Especially if he showed up in uniform. It was most women's kryptonite. I swear, my fourth-grade teacher even drooled when he entered the room one time. (Talk about embarrassing)

RAVEN:

So... did you confront him?

LIZZY:

He has no idea I was there... and none of you
had better tell him either.

LANIE:

Yeah, I'm not touching THAT with a ten-foot
pole!

SLOANE:

Hard pass for me... Not my monkey or circus.

RAVEN:

I can see it now... sitting him down for the
birds and bees talk, the way he tried with us
as teens. (laughing emoji)

LANIE:

Maybe we just start filling his drawers with
condoms???

SLOANE:

With our luck, one of our unsuspecting kids
would find them first, and he'd have a lot of
explaining to do.

RAVEN:

I for one am happy for him. He deserves to
find someone.

SLOANE:

As long as he's happy, all the power—and
great sex—to him.

LANIE:

Agreed. If it's someone worth bringing
around, I'm sure he will in due time.

SLOANE:

Now I'm dying to find out who Faye is!

RAVEN:

Ditto.

LIZZY:

Same... Look, I've done my due diligence—y'all have been warned not to go over unannounced. If you walk in on anything like what I did, don't say I didn't warn you.

# Chapter 20
## Mark



This is taking longer than expected. We'll finish tomorrow at 0700. I've rebooked the hotel. There's a room reserved in your name.

Seconds later, a confirmation link comes through.

Well, shit, I was hoping we'd fly out tonight.



Roger that. Need a ride?

I've got our rental car since Riggs has been in meetings at the Pentagon most of the day. I have to say, it's weird sitting idle. For years, I was seated at the table where decisions are made. Now, I'm stuck in limbo, twiddling my thumbs and waiting on others for orders to come through.

Usually, I have no problem staying busy. But this time, I'm not sure what to do with myself. I've done my best to stay occupied while remaining close, in case Riggs makes the call to leave. It's both a blessing and a curse to be demoted to transport detail, but such is life.

RIGGS:

No need. Just enjoy a free evening in DC. I'll text you when I have an update.

ME:

You know where to find me.

I've already spent most of my day doing mundane tasks. I've worked out, researched some potential clients for Riggs, and checked in with my family throughout the day. Being three hours ahead of Faye, I know better than to call and be a distraction. When we spoke this morning, she mentioned she'd be working on a big project and would text when her day is done.

She's on a tight deadline and needs to ensure her new program works before launching it with her latest client. Even though my brain knows this, my fingers itch to put through a call, simply so I can hear her voice.

*Gah, I'm a selfish bastard.*

I miss her like crazy.

If I go to my hotel room, my willpower will wane.

*Think—there's gotta be something I can do to distract myself.*

What's gotten into me? Why do I feel like a long-tailed cat in a room full of rockers? It's like Faye's put a spell on me, and I can barely go five minutes without thinking of her.

For Christ's sake, I've spent the better part of my adult life being single. I know how to be alone. I've never been one to let a woman distract me like this. So, why do I feel like a fish out of water now that I get an impromptu paid vacation?

Hell, I should be living it up.

DC was my stomping ground for nearly a year when I did a short tour at Andrews Air Force Base. I love this town. So, why can't I just relax and enjoy this time away?

*It shouldn't be this hard.*

Food is the last thing on my mind, since I ate a late lunch, thinking I'd be flying most of the evening. Our rental is already parked in a garage nearby, and I'd rather not fight traffic at this hour. Maybe I can quickly head to my hotel and check in, then go out on foot and see what there is to do here in the Adams Morgan neighborhood.

AN HOUR LATER, I'm strolling down 20th Street, making my way to Dupont Circle. The sidewalk is crowded. Some are dodging one another as they hurry to get home after a long day's work, while others are linked arm in arm with their significant other, enjoying this warm summer afternoon in DC without a care in the world. Those who are holding hands stop and window shop on their way to their next destination.

When a jogger shouts, "On your left," from behind, I dodge right to avoid a couple stopping to look at something on their phone in front of me.

That's when I see it.

The shimmering glint of blue that reminds me of Faye's eyes.

Needing a closer look, I step toward the window, and I'm instantly transported to that day all those years ago, when everything about my feelings for Faye changed.

*We were in Seattle, heading to a concert, and something in a shop nearby had caught her attention. Since we were holding hands, I abruptly stopped alongside her.*

*"What are we stopping for?" I innocently asked.*

*"Look at that blue sapphire," she gasped in awe. "It's gorgeous."*

*Glancing from the ring to her, I remember thinking, Not*

nearly as gorgeous as you. *But instead, I said something along the lines of, "It's almost the color of your eyes."*

"Someday... when I get engaged," she'd whispered in awe, "I want a ring like that."

"Uh... Don't most girls want diamonds?" I'd teased.

"That's what makes this special, Mark. Not only is it my birthstone, but it would show me the man who wants to spend the rest of my life with me knows the real me. One of the only gifts I remember from my grandmother is a pair of blue sapphire earrings, in this exact shade. They are my most prized possession."

"Really?"

"Yes, before she passed, she brought me into her bedroom one day, and we were looking at her jewelry. My grandfather loved to surprise her with gifts from time to time. After she laid them all out for me to see, she asked which one was my favorite."

Sighing heavily, she placed her free hand over her heart. "I remember there was a diamond necklace and earrings, and a few other gemstones on various matching sets. But the one that stood out was the pair of blue sapphire earrings."

"Did she give them to you that day?"

"No, I didn't know it at the time, but it was her way of setting up her will. She let me wear those earrings at my eighth-grade graduation. Then, when she passed about a year later, she gifted them to me, along with a letter I'll always cherish."

"Wow," I said, speechless.

"A ring like this would match perfectly with my earrings." She'd sighed heavily. "I want something to represent my past, present, and future with my future husband. That's why a traditional wedding band will never work."

When I'm bumped from behind, I'm brought back to the present.

For the longest time, I stare at the vintage white gold ring in the display case. A large radiant-cut blue sapphire is set in the center, with two smaller diamonds flanking each side.

Faye and I most certainly have a past.

She's occupying nearly every thought of my present.

After reconnecting, I hope like hell we have a future together.

"Yo, buddy, you goin' in or out?" An impatient man stands to my left, hoping to enter the door I'm blocking.

Glancing once more to the ring in front of me, then up to the sky for guidance, I make a split decision.

One I hope I don't live to regret.

# Chapter 21
## Faye

It's late when I finally feel I'm at a stopping point with this project. As I shut down my computer, I stand and stretch my aching limbs. Taking off my glasses, I rub at my dry eyes and head to my room to change into pajamas.

When I finally pick up my phone, I see there are several missed messages.

One from my mom, just checking in.

I'll call her back in the morning.

Another from a client, asking to set up a meeting later next week.

Again, it's not pressing, so I'll deal with it tomorrow.

The last came through about an hour ago.

MARK:

Hey, sweetheart, just checking in. Riggs has another meeting in the morning, so we're staying another night. I'm at my hotel room. Call me when you're free.

Shit, it's nearly midnight there.

Not wanting to wake him, I send a quick text.

ME:

> Sorry. Got lost in the zone. Just now checking messages. Don't want to wake you if you're sleeping.

Within seconds, the phone rings, and my heart soars like a teenager with her first crush at seeing his name.

"Hey, you." I smile in greeting as I connect the call. "How's your trip?"

"Better now that I hear your voice. Can we switch to a video call? I miss your beautiful face."

"Sure." I laugh at his eagerness.

Within seconds, his handsome face fills my phone. A playful smile pulls at his lips. "God, you're even better looking than I remember."

"You're not so bad yourself, handsome," I tease, though something settles in me when my eyes finally meet his.

"How's your project going?" he asks with interest.

"Almost done. When I bring this client on board, I'll travel to Bologna to get this up and running."

Mark's brows draw together, and the phone tilts to the side for a moment before he asks, "How soon will you leave?"

"Not for another week or so. I'm still troubleshooting a few things before I make the trip, or it will all be for nothing."

I watch him settle onto his bed and lean against the headboard. "Will you be gone long?"

"Not sure. The last time I did something like this, I was gone six weeks. The time before, it only took two. It all depends on what I encounter when I get there."

"Hmmm... That must be hard to plan around. Are all jobs like this?"

Shaking my head, I sigh heavily and settle onto my bed, as

well. "No, thankfully. I try to limit how many clients like this I take. Fortunately, most of what I do can be done remotely, so it only happens a couple of times a year. Otherwise, I'd never be home."

"I can certainly relate," he says solemnly.

Something in the way he says it has me taking a closer look at his features.

His usually sculpted hair stands on end, as if he's repeatedly been running a hand through it. There are dark circles under his eyes that I've rarely noticed before, and he's looking at me with a sense of need I can't quite describe.

"Everything okay, Mark?"

"Yeah," he sighs heavily. "This trip is just... different for me." Then, a slow grin spreads across his face. "For some reason... I've been rather preoccupied. I can't seem to get my mind off a certain someone, and I'm jonesing to get home."

From the suddenly heated look in his eyes, I know without a doubt he's talking about me, and my heart does a somersault into my belly. But I can't let him off that easily. "I imagine you miss your family a lot when you're gone."

"Yes, I do," he says flatly. "But from that glint in your eye, I can tell you know damn well I wasn't talking about them."

"All joking aside, what makes this trip different?" I ask with genuine curiosity.

Mark's head shakes slightly. "I'm not sure. For years, I've been deployed, have gone on quick missions, and even been stationed out of reach of my family for months on end. But this little in-and-out I'm doing for Riggs hits different."

"Is it because you're getting used to being with your girls now?" I suggest.

A long and steady breath escapes as he just stares into the phone.

When I don't say anything, he eventually rolls his lower lip under his teeth and shakes his head slowly. "Truth?" He finally shrugs.

"No, lie to me. It always works out *so* well that way," I playfully snark.

"God, you are adorable when you're being a brat." He chuckles, then he quickly adds, "This right here is why I blame you, Faye."

"Me? What did I do?" I guffaw in defense.

Rolling his eyes, he smirks adorably. "You made me fall for you."

"Good to know I'm not the only one, Lancaster. I'm a master at compartmentalization. Otherwise, I wouldn't get a thing done now that I know you're living next door."

"I used to be the same way... until now. I swear, it's like my feelings for you all those years ago just lay dormant and were revitalized with a vengeance the second I saw you again. Only this time, I'm an adult and know better than to dismiss them."

If that doesn't hit like a ton of bricks, I'm not sure what else would.

"Wait... Dismiss them? What are you talking about?"

"I'm saying..." He pauses to readjust the phone that's propped up in front of him. Once he settles, he continues, "I was in love with you when you pushed me away all those years ago."

"I—" I start, but he cuts me off.

"If you *hadn't* pushed me away, I wouldn't have my girls or my career, for that matter. Don't get me wrong, I wouldn't change any of it for the world. I love them to the ends of the earth. I have zero regrets. I'm a firm believer in everything happening for a reason."

"Then what is it?" I ask, not following his train of thought.

"In just a week of having you back in my life, I know without a doubt, I've never loved anyone the way I love you.

Yes, I loved Sarah, to a point... After all, she's the mother of my children. I'll always be grateful to her. But there's a reason it fizzled out eventually."

Tears prick the back of my eyes as I listen to him declare his love for me.

"Faye, you are truly the only person I've ever been completely, 1000 percent, irrevocably in love with."

"Oh, Mark..." I sigh. My chest tightens from my heart growing so big that it can barely contain itself. My throat thickens, and I can't process enough words to adequately explain my feelings for this wonderfully sexy and direct man.

One of the things I love most about him is that I've never had to wonder where I stand with him.

*Holy shit, this man loves me—just as much as I love him.*

As if he can sense I'm struggling to find the words, he arches a brow and says, "I'm hoping you're on the same page because if you feel even an ounce of what I do for you, I'm telling you now, I'm all in."

For the longest time, all I can do is stare.

A million thoughts fly through my head, but I only land on one.

"Ditto, Mark." Finally, the words come out in a whisper. "We're on the same page."

A wicked grin plays at his lips, and his fingers steeple under his chin. "That just leaves us with one minor little thing."

"What's that?" I'm confused by his expression.

"It's time you met my wonderful, wild, and chaotic family."

"Oh, no pressure there," I deadpan.

# Chapter 22
## Mark

It's early when I return to Seaside, and I'm starving. I've just flown a red eye, getting Riggs to PDX and myself back to Seaside. I'm tired, cranky, and in desperate need of food at this hour.

Not in the mood to cook, I pull into the diner shortly after it opens. True to form, there are already cars filling the parking lot. As I back my truck into a spot for an easy escape route, I think I see Jack Murdock's truck over to the side. I wonder if I'll see Ryan this morning, too. Ryan's less apt to stop in because he likes to help Lanie with the kids most mornings, but since it's summer, he might let them sleep in.

As the bell jingles above the door to signal my entrance, Martha greets me with a welcoming smile. "Well, look who the cat dragged in. Haven't seen you around lately."

"Just got back into town," I grumble.

"Want the usual?" she asks, walking me to a booth in the back corner of her section.

"Sure. A bacon and cheese omelet with a side of sourdough toast will hit the spot," I reply, rubbing my stomach. I can't wait for that coffee she'll bring to wash it down. There's no way I'll make it through the day without it.

As I pass by a booth filled with older men, I swear I'm hallucinating when I hear Faye's voice call out, "Mark?"

Turning around, I come face-to-face with the most gorgeous woman on the planet. Mouth gaping and wide-eyed, her deep blue eyes stare at me as if she, too, is in disbelief and doesn't trust I'm actually standing here in front of her.

Without hesitation, I swoop her into my arms and crash my lips on hers.

She tastes like heaven and home all wrapped into one.

The moment she links her arms around my neck and kisses me back, everything is right in my world. I instantly feel complete. My sour mood evaporates on the spot, and my only need is the woman in my arms.

Eventually, a loud throat clearing brings me back to reality.

*Fuck, we're in public, and I completely devoured her like a tall glass of water on a hot summer day.*

Reluctantly, I let Faye go, only to hear a familiar man's deep voice deadpan, "I thought something had been off with you lately; now I know why."

Reaching for her hand, I turn to face not only Jack and Ryan Murdock, but her dad, Mr. Ames. They're all seated in the booth next to us. Each with a different shocked expression on their face.

Well, shit. The cat's out of the bag now.

As I stiffen my shoulders and look them each in the eye, Faye awkwardly lets go of my hand and feigns excitement by using freaking jazz hands to announce, "Surprise. Mark's back in town... And well... obviously, we've reconnected."

Ryan's eyes widen, and his brows nearly lift off his face, but I'll give the guy credit; he doesn't say anything.

To her dad, she says, "Guess who moved in next door and has been doing all those renovations?"

"You don't say," her dad guffaws, as his hand slaps the table in front of him.

Reaching out for his hand to shake, I finally remember my manners. "It's good to see you, Mr. Ames."

From the corner of my eye, I catch Ryan covering his mouth and his shoulders shake in silent laughter.

*Oh, how the tables have turned.*

Ryan was nervous as fuck around me the first time we met, and now, he's watching my grown ass squirm like he did, until he learned I meant him no harm.

Shaking my hand stiffly, Mr. Ames smirks. "What... I don't get a greeting like that? I have to say, Faye, this guy sure knows how to put on a show. I think he made sweet Martha blush with a kiss like that."

*Kill. Me. Now.*

Ryan finally loses all hope of having any control and audibly rocks with laughter at my expense. His dad is doing the best he can to hold back his amusement but fails miserably, as well.

"Dad," Faye admonishes and swats at his arm. "Behave."

"I wasn't the one putting the moves on my baby girl in public. Serves him right to be in the hot seat. Just how long has this been going on?"

Before she can respond, Martha interjects, "Do you want me to bring your food to this table, Casanova?"

*Jeez—I'm never gonna hear the end of this.*

"We'll make room for him here," Jack Murdock states as he stands and grabs a chair from an empty table.

Mr. Ames and Faye slip back into their side of the booth, and I take the hot seat at the end of the table. When my knee bumps hers, Faye reaches for my hand and squeezes it tight.

Instantly, my body relaxes.

"So..." Mr. Ames starts once we're all settled, "has this been going on long?"

Again, Ryan covers his mouth and suddenly is very interested in his cup of coffee.

As a dad who happened to be a colonel in the Air Force, I'll admit, it was sometimes entertaining to put all the guys wanting to date any of my daughters on notice. Being the guy on the other end of that script, clearly interested in dating this man's daughter, it's not nearly as entertaining.

Faye and I are grown adults, and I certainly have nothing to hide.

Clearing my throat, I look him straight in the eye. "We ran into one another a little over a week ago."

Mr. Ames quirks a brow and smirks at his daughter. "Does this have anything to do with that time you had ants in your pants and called me bright and early, itching to get out of your house?"

When Faye nods with a shrug, Mr. Ames shakes his head and grimaces to himself. "I knew something was off that day. Your panties were all in a twist. You were jumping at everyone who walked through the door, and I couldn't for the life of me figure out why." Locking eyes with his daughter, he points to me. "I presume this fella was the reason?"

"We'd bumped into each other the day before."

Suddenly, his attention turns to me. "So, does this mean you're back in town for good?"

"Yes, sir. I'm here because my daughters and their families are here."

Mr. Ames darts his eyes from me to Ryan. "Oh, that's right. He's your son-in-law. He and Lanie have the cutest kids."

"Yes, they sure do," Jack muses as he reaches for his mug of coffee.

"It's a small world." Ryan smirks, still not looking me in the eye.

"And it keeps getting smaller," Mr. Ames agrees.

"Okay..." Faye interjects. "It's a small world. We all get it. Mark and I are seeing one another, and it's time to get on with it."

Shaking his head, Mr. Ames chuckles in delight. "Your mom is gonna be pissed she didn't make it to breakfast. She missed the tea of the century for this small town."

"We're not that big of a deal," Faye huffs in annoyance.

"*Oh, this is pretty big*," Ryan says under his breath as he sits up straighter in the booth.

Thankfully, Martha comes to deliver their food, and all is forgotten, for now.

"I'll be right back with yours, Mark. Can I get you some coffee?"

"Yes, please," I plead.

My adrenaline may have me on full alert now, but once my nerves settle from this little escapade, I'm sure I'll be crashing once again.

When everyone's occupied with their meal, Faye leans toward me and asks, "When did you get back?"

"I drove straight here from the airport. I didn't expect you to be up."

"We like to grab breakfast once a week or so," Mr. Ames interjects before taking a bite of his pancake.

"I'm surprised we never ran into one another," I wonder aloud.

"Dad, you know Mom likes to monitor your meals. She only lets you get away with coming to town because she thinks I'll do her job for her."

This earns Faye a grimace. "I can handle myself just fine, thank you very much."

Faye puts her hands up and surrenders. "You're the one who underwent heart surgery. You can deal with her wrath if you don't want to stick to your diet."

"I stick to my diet. But an occasional piece of bacon won't hurt me."

Wanting to help the guy out, I interject and change the subject. "Hey, Ryan, do you think Lanie and the kids would be up for a bonfire tonight? I'd been promising them one for a while, and with the forecast, tonight might be the best shot we have for the next week or so."

"I'm fairly certain we're free, but I'll double-check." Ryan digs out his phone and presumably texts his wife.

Within a few seconds, he looks up from his phone and grins. "We're good. Want me to mention it in the family group chat? I pretty sure everyone's back in town, including Sloane."

"Saves me the trouble." I shrug. Then, to the rest of the table, I add, "You're all more than welcome to join us."

Looking at Faye, I squeeze her hand, hoping she, of all people, will attend.

I know I should've cleared my sudden plans with her first, but as I glance her way, she smiles in reassurance. Besides, she's already agreed to meet my girls. With Ryan being a first-hand witness to my kissing the hell out of her just a few moments ago, it's probably best not to put their meeting off any longer.

"Thanks for the offer," Jack says, "but we've got a chamber of commerce dinner tonight."

Faye's dad simply shakes his head. "No can do. Your mom and I are playing pinochle with the Starkweathers. You know how much Lisa and Roy love their games. We'll catch you another time."

As my plate of food is brought to the table, Ryan looks up and grins. "Everyone's in for the bonfire. The girls want to know what to bring."

"Tell them I'll text the group once we're done eating," I say, before taking my first bite of omelet.

My stomach grumbles in anticipation, and Faye's beautiful laughter fills the room. "When was the last time you've eaten?"

"Last night before we took off," I admit.

"Hmmm..." she muses as she takes a bite of her waffle. "And *you* get after *me* for skipping meals."

Conversation picks up around the table, and I spend the next few minutes devouring my plate.

Eventually, while everyone is occupied, she leans over and whispers so only I can hear. "I finished my project late last night, so I've got a few days free. Think I can persuade you into hanging out with me?"

"Sweetheart, that's something you'll never have to ask me twice. As soon as we finish eating, are you ready to get out of here?"

# Chapter 23
## Sisters Group Chat



LANIE:

Ladies… Make sure you're seated and buckle up! You're never gonna believe what I just heard.

LANIE:

I'd also advise swallowing any drinks before reading further… Have I got a story to tell you.

LIZZY:

What are you talking about?

LANIE:

The mystery has been solved!!!

SLOANE:

Dramatic much?

LIZZY:

Just tell us already! (A woman impatiently tapping her foot gif)

LANIE:

Word on the street is Dad got caught kissing the hell out of Herb Ames's daughter.

SLOANE:

Who is Herb Ames?

LANIE:

Wait for it… Her name is…

LIZZY:

For crying out loud… just tell us already!

LANIE:

Faye!

LIZZY:

What are you talking about? And how do you know he was kissing her?

LANIE:

Ryan saw it firsthand at the diner. Apparently, Dad walked in, Faye called his name, and as Ryan says, Dad turned around, and I quote, "kissed the ever-loving hell out of her." He was so consumed, he didn't even notice Ryan sitting in the booth next to him, or her dad, of all people, trying to get their attention.

SLOANE:

Shut up. He did not. (heads exploding emoji)

LANIE:

He did. Then Ryan watched him have his ass handed to him the way he terrified all of our husbands when they met Dad for the first time. Ryan nearly died on the spot. Karma came full circle for Colonel Lancaster. Apparently, it was epic, and we missed it!

RAVEN:

Holy shit... I missed the motherlode of gossip. Wait. When did this happen?

LANIE:

This morning at the diner. Keep up.

RAVEN:

Sorry. Some of us are still working this summer and have deadlines.

SLOANE:

I'm working, and I still responded.

RAVEN:

Yeah, yeah, overachiever. (eye roll emoji)

LIZZY:

So, Dad's officially dating this woman? Or did he just kiss her?

LANIE:

According to Ryan, she declared to the entire diner that they're back together.

RAVEN:

Holy shit. This is huge!

LIZZY:

Have they been dating long?

LANIE:

It's new. Apparently, they reconnected last week.

RAVEN:

Reconnected? It must be serious if he greeted her with a kiss like that.

SLOANE:

That follows the timeline of my boys' stories about her. Apparently, she's made quite an impression on more than one Lancaster. They still talk about how much fun she was.

LIZZY:

Does that mean she'll be at the bonfire tonight?

LANIE:

From my understanding, yes.

SLOANE:

I can't wait to meet her. She sounds like a lot of fun.

LIZZY:

Should we let on that we know? Or be surprised?

LANIE:

Dad knows Ryan and I hardly keep secrets.

RAVEN:

He'd be a fool to think Ryan wouldn't blab about something like this.

SLOANE:

Dad's no fool. Just be nice so she'll stick around.

LIZZY:

No kidding. Our family can be a lot for someone new. Especially, since we've multiplied like rabbits over the last few years.

SLOANE:

Wait... Does she have any kids?

LANIE:

I have no idea.

RAVEN:

Guess we'll wait and see.

SLOANE:

Be sure to put in the family group chat what you're bringing. Dad just texted. He's taking requests and is heading to the store this afternoon.

LIZZY:

Sounds good. Gotta run. Embry's trying to ride a skateboard in the house.

RAVEN:

You can blame Dad for that one.

SLOANE:

Just wait until he's cruising down the promenade. See if your heart can handle it.

LIZZY:

See you tonight. Wish me luck!

# Chapter 24
## Faye

Mark assures me I have nothing to be nervous about, but that's like telling me not to breathe. Sure, I've met his parents before —and for the record, his mother loved me— but I've never met a man's kids.

Hell, Mark doesn't just have four girls I need to impress. No, he has an entire gaggle of grandkids and sons-in-law, some of whom are world famous, who will all be wondering what the hell I'm doing, intruding on their family gathering.

As I look in the mirror a final time, I force myself to stare into my own eyes.

"Stop worrying. You've got this," I tell myself.

Even as my stomach flips with nerves, I straighten my shoulders, grab my favorite hoodie, and walk out the door to meet Mark at his place.

After coming home from the diner, he and I spent most of the day in his bed. Then, about two hours ago, he forced himself to go to the store and pick up the necessary items for tonight's adventure. I heard his truck pull in next door a few minutes ago, and now that I no longer look as if I've been ravaged by him all day, I force myself to leave the comforts of my home and join him.

By the time I get outside, he's already walking my way. "You ready?" he asks with a handsome, carefree smile on his face.

"As ready as I'll ever be," I admit with a nervous laugh.

Leaning in, he reaches for my hand and kisses my cheek. "Don't worry, Faye. They'll love you."

"How can you be so sure?" I hedge.

"Because *I* love you..." He squeezes my hand and leads me toward his garage.

As much as I want to protest, I know this self-doubt is just my nerves talking. I may not win them all over at once, but at least two of his grandkids and I got along well. If the rest are anything like Jason and Josh, I'm sure I'm worrying for nothing.

---

TWENTY MINUTES LATER, we're pulling up to Lanie and Ryan's house—though to me, it will always be Jane Lancaster's home. An odd sense of déjà vu comes over me. I feel like he's bringing me home to meet his mom for the first time, rather than meet his four daughters and their entire family. Suddenly, I miss Jane like crazy. I always cherished the time we spent together and wish we'd been able to visit more often over the years.

As Mark takes his hand in mine, he leads me up the front steps, and my stomach feels like a swarm of hornets taking flight. When we walk through the door, flashbacks of Jane's warm scent overwhelm me.

"How does it still smell the same?" I ask in disbelief as he leads me into the front hall.

Mark squeezes my hand and chuckles. "You'll have to ask Ryan about his little mishap when ordering Mom's favorite air freshener. I'm fairly certain they've got a lifetime supply. Ha. Since this is now his home, he gets to live with it. I guess that's the price he's paying for trying to impress Lanie."

"Hmmm, that sounds like quite a story," I muse with laughter.

"Oh, it is... Trust me. Just ask Lanie about it one day when Ryan's not around. You'll get the full scoop."

Inhaling deeply, Jane's familiar scent somehow calms my nerves, and I'm suddenly ready to face her enormous family. She'd always hoped she'd have an even bigger one than her two children and four granddaughters. I always loved her stories about the girls, and now that I'm finally meeting them, it feels like I've come full circle.

The sound of little feet slapping down the hall draws me out of my trip down memory lane. "Papa... Faye... You're here!" Two familiar boys come charging at us.

One clings to Mark, as the other collides into me and hugs me so tight, he almost knocks me over. It takes a second to recover, but instinctually, I squeeze my surprise hugger back just as hard. When he pulls back, I see it's Jason. "Hey, Jay. It's good to see you."

Turning to his brother, he grins. "See... I told ya she'd know."

Hands to his hip, Josh asks, "How'd ya know, Faye? We usually trick everyone new."

Instantly, I relax even further as I chuckle at the twins' antics. "Well, for starters, your voice is a little different. The second"—I look from Jason to Josh playfully—"is my little secret. If I let you know my superpowers, you'll get away with everything."

Thank God, Josh has a tiny freckle above his left eye, or I'd never have been able to tell them apart.

"No, we won't." Josh sighs heavily, "Because you're like Momma and won't let us get away with nothin'.'"

"What won't I let you get away with?" a woman, I assume is Sloane, says, rounding the corner.

Jason rolls his eyes at his brother and points a thumb at me. "Faye has superpowers like you and can tell us apart."

As I reach out my hand in greeting, Sloane bypasses it and pulls me in for a hug. "It's so nice to finally meet you. My boys haven't stopped talking about their new friend Faye since they've been home." When she pulls back, she gasps. "Wait... You're the one in the picture."

"What?" Mark and I say in unison.

"Nana has a picture right here in the hall of you and another girl out on the beach when you were kids. I thought it was one of Aunt Mable's friends, but now that I've seen you in person, I know it's you, Faye."

Another girl, who is the spitting image of Sloane, steps into the hall and joins us. If I were a betting woman, I'd put my money on it being Raven. Even as adults, they're identical. However, Raven now has a tattoo on her inner wrist and an edgier look to her than she did as a teen.

"Raven, you know that picture of Dad, Mable, and that girl we never knew the name of on the beach, that's right over there...?" She points to a framed photo on the wall.

"Yes..." Raven's brows pull tight. "What about it?"

"It's Faye. Nana said it was Dad's first crush, but never gave us her name."

"I always thought he was crushing on one of Aunt Mable's friends." Then she looks between her dad and me and smirks, just like I've seen Mark do a million times. "But obviously, the two of you were *more than friends* back in the day."

Sloane quirks a brow. "At least that's the word on the street."

"You say that like we're not even here," Mark grumbles.

"What are y'all doing in the hall?" another of Mark's daughters asks as she comes into view. If I had to guess, it's Melanie, or Lanie, as everyone calls her. Jane used to show me pictures and tell me so many stories about these girls, I feel as if I already know them.

"Hi, I'm Faye." I reach out to shake her hand in greeting. "You must be Lanie?" I guess, hoping I didn't make the wrong assumption.

"Wow... she's good," Josh pipes in. "Papa, did you give her a cheat sheet, like our video games?"

Mark's deep chuckle fills the room. "No, buddy, I didn't." Then he turns to me and asks, "How *are* you doing this?"

"Let's go into the living room so we all can hear her explanation," Lanie suggests, ushering this suddenly large gathering out of the hall.

Once we're settled, Raven asks, "So, how is it you're able to tell us apart?"

Looking at Mark, I shrug. "First, your dad and I were the best of friends growing up. Which means I was also close to your nana, as she liked to be called."

"Really?" Ryan asks in disbelief. "Talk about a small world."

"Yeah, I suppose it is," I muse, then continue. "After your dad joined the Air Force, Jane and I remained close friends. I visited her as often as I visited my own parents over the years. My parents are Herb and Virgie Ames. I'm sure you've met them at some point. Your grandmother loved playing cards with them after Mark moved away."

"But how the heck can you tell everyone apart?" Mark prompts. "I know *we've* certainly never talked about it."

"Jane." I grin widely as I look around the room. "She used to bring out her infamous photo albums and tell me stories about your girls every time I visited. Thankfully, you haven't changed that much since you were teenagers, so once the boys pointed out Sloane as their mom, the rest kinda fell in line like dominoes."

When the sliding door glides open, and Jax Cartwright comes in, I feel my breath catch in my chest. It's surreal to see someone I've seen perform countless times on social media waltz right into Jane's home.

"The fire's made. Who's gonna go out and enjoy it with me?"

Pandemonium ensues as everyone jumps up from their seat around the living room and makes their way out to the bonfire on the beach. Throughout all the chaos, Lizzy, her husband, and three children arrive to join us.

Mark had already dropped off the juice, soda, hot dogs, and marshmallows before coming to pick me up, so apparently, there's nothing to do but go out and enjoy ourselves at the beach.

As we head outside, Mark pulls me to a stop between two sand dunes where no one can see us and asks, "You doing all right?"

"Yeah. Your family is wonderful," I admit. "I'm not sure what I was so nervous about."

"I told you it would all work out." His sexy smirk makes me want to kiss that smug look right off his face, but alas, we're not alone.

"I completely forgot that your picture has been hanging on Mom's wall for years. I'm surprised they made the connection, though."

"Well... Apparently, your mom thought enough to tell them

you had a crush on me," I tease playfully. "Who knew I left such an impression?"

"You know damn well I've had more than a crush on you for years, Faye," Mark says, leaning in to kiss me.

*Ah, this is just what I need to calm my nerves.*

Before I can get consumed by him, I hear my name. "Faye, you coming? I wanna sit by you at the fire."

"Was that Jason or Josh?" I whisper so they won't hear.

Mark's amused expression melts my heart. "How the hell would I know?"

"I can only tell them apart if I see their foreheads..." I admit with a laugh. "If Josh didn't have that freckle, I'd never know."

"What freckle?" Mark laughs. "I always watch the way they walk or smile."

As we walk over the last dune, I'm surprised by the setup this family has. Not only is there a large fire, blankets and chairs already set out, but there's a small half-dome-shaped shelter with a large tarp attached to the bottom set up on one side, where two girls are playing with dolls. Some kids are digging in the sand with beach toys, while others race back and forth between lines they've drawn in the sand. Their dads stand nearby with drinks in their hands, chatting about something to one another, as Mark's daughters gather around the fire, sitting in chairs or on blankets.

I've quickly been forgotten as the twins play with their cousins.

"Over here, Faye," Lanie calls out. "Dad can help watch the kids while we catch up."

"If that doesn't sound like a lamb being led to the slaughter, I don't know what does," I mutter.

Looking at Mark, he squeezes my hand in reassurance.

"Go ahead... They won't bite," he teases. "But fair warning, they *will* dig into your past relentlessly... So be careful what you reveal." Then he whispers, "Oh... If you tell any of my girls, I'll deny it, but I truly think they each missed their calling as detectives."

Before I can respond, one of his younger granddaughters calls out, "Papa, come help us dig. We need a deep hole around this castle."

"Okay, Vivy. I'll be right there." Before he heads off to help, his eyes lock onto mine. "You good?"

"I'm good." I quickly nod, then make my way over to his daughters.

When I get there, Lizzy offers, "Would you like something to drink? We've got wine, soda, and water."

"If you choose wine, we've got tumblers to keep the sand out," Lanie interjects, holding a cup out to me. "We just opened the best Moscato."

"Moscato, it is." I grin, then take a seat on the empty blanket beside them.

"So..." Raven claps, then grins conspiratorially. "I'm dying to know... How old were you when you and Dad started dating the first time?"

This earns a loud roar of laughter from the entire group.

When they settle, I say, "As I said, we were the best of friends for years before we started dating. Hmmm... I think things changed the summer between our sophomore and junior year."

"Wait," Lizzy gasps, "That was *you* in his prom photo. I remember he was wearing a purple tie, and you had a really pretty dark-purple dress. Nana showed it to me once when we were looking for something in her craft room. She found it in a box."

"Yeah, we went to both junior and senior prom together," I reveal, taking the sealed teal tumbler from Raven when she hands it to me.

"Forget vintage Dad." Raven snorts out a laugh as she nearly drops her sunglasses; she's leaning so far forward in her chair. "I'm dying to know how the two of you reconnected *this* time?"

"Uh... Don't get your hopes up, as it's far from cute or glamorous," I scoff in warning.

"Even so, we'd like to know... if you're willing to share," Sloane prods.

"Ladies, I caught your father's attention again..." I draw out, giving a theatric pause, then go for the punchline, "while taking out the trash early one morning... Glamorous, I know. My can nearly got stuck in a rut, and it drew his attention."

"Uh..." Raven draws out, clearly unimpressed.

Before any of them can say anything, I continue, "Then he disappeared for three days and showed up, expecting to take me to dinner. No warning, no invitation, just a knock on my door."

"Yeah, that sounds like Dad." Lanie sighs heavily. "He's so used to commanding battalions, he often forgets he's around civilians."

"He hasn't been that bad," I quickly assure them. "In fact, he was quite flexible the night we watched movies with the twins."

"He can be... until he starts making plans. Then he forgets we're not nearly as regimented as him," Raven points out. "He's getting better now that he's retired, but you can't teach an old dog like him too many new tricks."

"Good to see he hasn't changed much over the years." I laugh. "Though your nana was much the same way, so he came by it honestly."

"Really?" Lizzy asks in disbelief. "She was always so go-with-the-flow with us, growing up."

"Probably because we outnumbered her four-to-one,"

Raven deadpans in a tone that reminds me so much of her father.

"That, and she didn't have to be the heavy, if our parents were around," Lanie says, rolling her eyes.

Suddenly, their gaggle of kids screeches in laughter. Our attention is drawn to their dads and grandfather chasing them in circles through the sand. Once they're caught, they're carried like human footballs under each arm until another can be nabbed. Then, they're swapped out once both arms are full. My heart warms at the pure joy radiating on both the kids' and the grown men's faces. Their smiles are infectious, and my cheeks ache as I watch them.

*Mark is so lucky to have this.*

When they settle, I probe, "Okay... So I don't get caught in the lurch, someone please fill me in on who all these kids are. I've gotta keep the twins thinking I've got these magical superpowers they claim I miraculously have, and stay one step ahead of them."

"Well, for starters, they're not the only set of twins," Raven warns. "My two girls, Vivian and Savannah, are over there, chasing my husband." She points to the girls chasing Finn McGowen, whom I recognize as the drummer for Ruby Frax.

If I had to guess, I'd say they're nearly the age of Jason and Josh. Raven interrupts my cataloging when she adds another tidbit of information. "Though we typically call them Vivy and Vanny. Vivy's wearing yellow."

"Good to know." I smile as I watch them each get snatched by their dad and giggle with delight.

Then Lizzy chimes in. "Cameron's got our youngest of this brood, Embry, snagged under his arm, and they're chasing Jason and Josh. Over there, by Dad, is Milli, our oldest..." When we watch her sprinting away from Mark, Lizzy cheers, "Go, Milli! Don't let Papa catch you!"

"Hey... Whose side are you on?" Mark grumbles as she darts to his left just as he's about to snag her and misses.

"She's got moves, Papa! Watch out!" Lizzy taunts.

"I see how it is...." Mark zips to the right and snags another kid instead.

"That's Carter, my youngest." Lanie chuckles. "Poor guy, he didn't even see Dad coming."

"Gotta be quick on your feet when Dad's around. The man still runs miles each morning, for fun," Raven adds, then shouts, "Go, Candace, go! Papa's on your heels... Turn and burn, baby!"

For the next few minutes, our attention is on the impromptu game of chase. From what I gather, there's really no rhyme or reason to their chaos. The only thing that matters is they're having fun.

When the guys finally tucker all the kids out, they come over to join us.

It's Mark who declares, "Are you all ready for some dinner? I brought hot dogs, and Ryan's got our roasting sticks ready."

That's all it takes.

To my surprise, Jason and Josh both come to sit near me, ditching their parents. As the rest of the kids find places to sit further back from the flames, Ryan gives campfire skewers to Mark and each of the dads. Efficiently, Ryan passes out hot dogs to everyone once they're settled, and like a well-oiled machine, someone pulls out these Y-shaped spikes, and they're quickly bored into the sand to hold the skewers over the coals, which are perfect for roasting.

This is obviously not their first rodeo.

As Mark settles next to me, he leans in so that only I can hear and asks, "Still doin' okay?

"Yep." I grin as Jason scoots closer and reaches for my hand.

"I'm having a great time. Thanks for inviting me. I absolutely love your family."

"Good." Shifting closer, he whispers, "I know we're a wild and chaotic bunch at times, but I'm glad you're here to share this with me."

"Papa," Josh interrupts. "Is Faye your girlfriend?"

Mark reaches around me and tussles his hair playfully, "What do *you* know about girlfriends?"

My heart stalls, and my breath catches in my throat.

*There's no way I just heard him say that.*

When neither Mark nor I says anything, he continues matter-of-factly, "Momma said she was."

"Your momma's a smart woman," Mark muses. From that twitch of his lip, I can tell he's fighting like hell not to laugh.

"So... is she?" Josh pushes further, wide-eyed and expectant in learning the answer.

"Would it be a problem if she were?" Mark counters.

"No. Jay and I love her."

*Oh. My. Heart. He is just the sweetest boy ever.*

Mark leans in conspiratorially and whisper-shouts, "That's good, kiddo. Cuz I love her, too. Should we try keeping her?"

Both boys nod fervently.

Then Josh asks as if his papa hasn't just rocked my world, "Is my hot dog ready?

It's a good thing I'm sitting down, because between the two of them, I've been rendered speechless. Not only did they just completely steal my heart, but I'm not so sure I want it back. Mark must notice my shift in mood because he lifts an arm over me and pulls me in close. For the longest time, all I can do is lean into Mark and stare at the burning fire in front of me.

By the time everyone has their hot dog roasted and s'more eaten, it's getting dark. As I lean further into Mark on the blanket beside me, Jason falls asleep with his head on my lap.

"Hey, Dad," Sloane hollers, catching our attention, "Faye is the twin whisperer. Just look at what she's done to my boys." I glance down and smile at Josh who's fallen asleep leaning against Mark and myself. "You need to bring her around more often."

Squeezing me tight, I hear Mark's smile without even looking when he says, "Oh, I plan to, trust me."

# Chapter 25
## Sisters Group Chat

LANIE:

Last night was fun. We should do that again soon!

SLOANE:

No kidding. The boys loved it so much, they slept until almost nine! They haven't stopped talking about the bonfire since they got up.

RAVEN:

Mine too. It was the first thing Vanny asked about this morning.

LIZZY:

Embry has no clue what it means to sleep in. (crying emoji) If the sun is up, he is up.

LANIE:

Those days will soon pass, I promise. (heart emoji)

LIZZY:

Milli was the same way. She eventually learned to sleep in, so there's hope. (fingers crossed emoji)

RAVEN:

Speaking of hope... Anyone else notice how Dad was looking at Faye last night when he thought no one was watching?

LIZZY:

I think she's perfect for him!

LANIE:

Perfect for him? Hell, she's perfect for our entire family. Did you see the way she had Josh and Jason's number?

LIZZY:

Those two didn't know what to do with her "superpowers." It was hysterical.

LANIE:

She scored HUGE when she could tell us all apart.

SLOANE:

I for one was shocked to learn she didn't have any kids of her own. That woman is a miracle worker with my boys.

LIZZY:

Maybe we should adopt her and make her an honorary family member?

RAVEN:

Or...

RAVEN:

Hear me out...

RAVEN:

Dad could get off his ass…

RAVEN:

AND… make it OFFICIAL!!!

LANIE:

Jumping the gun much, Drama Queen? As much as I love Faye for him, I've NEVER in my life seen Dad date anyone. EVER! What makes you think he'll ask her to marry him???

RAVEN:

Just a feeling.

SLOANE:

If I'm being honest… I could see it. I mean, it wouldn't be such a bad thing. (shrugs emoji)

LIZZY:

He's literally only brought her around once. (head exploding emoji)

LANIE:

And with our crazy brood, we likely scared her off!

RAVEN:

Did you see them sneaking a kiss between the dunes when they thought no one was looking?

LANIE:

Yes! They were adorable. Ryan said it had nothing on the kiss he laid on her at the diner. So… the one at the diner must've been H-O-T!

LIZZY:

I always miss out on everything!

SLOANE:

You might've been changing Embry. When I noticed the first time, I didn't want to make a big deal of it. Raven might have a point. Dad's really into Faye.

LANIE:

He wasn't the only one with googly eyes all night. Those two were like teenagers trying to steal kisses when they thought no one was watching. It was adorable.

RAVEN:

He, of all people, should know better than to attempt to sneak around us… He's the one who taught us all how to spy on one another.

LANIE:

He did not!

LIZZY:

Oh, yes, he did. Once, I made fifty bucks for following Raven around town all night. He figured she couldn't get up to too much trouble with me in tow.

RAVEN:

Was that the time you offered to buy me ice cream?

LIZZY:

Yep. I was hungry and couldn't leave your sight. That boy you were hanging out with even paid when we got to the ice cream shop, so I scored! (Even though you didn't.)

RAVEN:

You did not just go there….

LANIE:

Face it, Raven, you were a heart attack waiting to happen for Dad.

SLOANE:

She's got you there. (shrugs emoji)

RAVEN:

THE POINT IS... (cough cough—focus, people) Dad is hooked on Faye, mark my words.

# Chapter 26
## Mark

I'm doing my best to pass the time while Faye's away in Italy. I've completed yet another project on my house. My guest bedrooms have now been freshly painted and redecorated, with input from both Faye and my girls.

Thank God for modern technology, like video conferencing, or I'd be a miserable jackass to everyone around me. It's been more than two weeks since I've seen her. I'm tired, cranky, and missing her far more than I expected. With the time difference, I've been burning the candle at both ends, trying to talk with her when she's available. Unfortunately, this project she's working on is taking longer than expected, as she's having both hardware and software issues since her client didn't fully upgrade their system before bringing her on board.

This also means I have no idea when I'll see her again in person.

I've just finished my second run for the day when I hear a knock at my door.

Knowing my kids have keys or can go through the garage, I

ignore it at first. Then the knock occurs again, so I get up from the barstool I'd been resting on and reluctantly answer it.

Expecting an unwanted solicitor, I'm surprised to find Herb Ames standing on my front porch.

"Mr. Ames," I say, my voice higher than usual, as I'm clearly shocked to see him standing in front of me.

"Oh, enough with that Mr. Ames crap." He swats at the air. "Call me Herb. It's been over thirty years, and you're a grown man now, son."

"Okay, Herb it is." I nod in agreement. Opening the door wider and gesturing for him to enter, I quickly add, "Come on in. Can I get you something to drink? I've got soda, beer, or I can make coffee if you'd like."

"Soda is fine," he says as he follows me to the kitchen.

"Have a seat." I gesture to the barstools and busy myself by pulling two cans of Pepsi from the fridge. "You want a glass or ice?"

"The can is fine," he says, reaching for it.

"You look like a man on a mission," I muse aloud. "What can I help you with?"

"I'm sorry to come over unannounced, but I don't have your number. Since I was watering Faye's plants, I thought I'd drop by."

"You're welcome here any time," I offer, wondering where he's going with this. Knowing he and Faye speak regularly, I point out, "You know... You can always get my number from Faye."

"I could." He shrugs, running a finger around the rim of his can. "But then she'd know we were talking."

This has me instantly on alert.

"What's going on, Herb?" I ask, as a litany of possible reasons spin through my mind.

Swatting at the air, much like his daughter does, he shakes

his head. "Can't a guy just want to talk with the man his daughter's seeing?"

"Okay..." I draw out. "You know you can. But I've got a feeling there's a particular reason you're dropping by unannounced."

"You've got me there, Mark. I know things between you and Faye are still fairly new... Well, at least since you've been reacquainted."

"True," I draw out, hoping he'll connect the dots for me as to why he's here, rather than make me guess at them.

Drawing in a heavy breath, he finally says, "Son, I'm gonna be frank with you."

"As you should," I encourage.

"I saw the way you looked at my daughter the other morning, and more importantly, the way she looked at you when she thought no one was watching her."

"Okay..." *Where the fuck is this going?*

"She loves you; it's as clear as day."

"And I love her," I point out. "Please make your point faster because I'm not sure I like where you're going with this."

He'd better not be here to ask me to stop seeing her. Losing her once was more than I'd ever want to endure in a lifetime.

"Ever since the two of you broke things off years ago, I've never seen Faye look at another man the way she's always looked at you. Her mother and I knew you were the one for her years ago. But we also know she was the one who pushed you away so you'd pursue your own dreams, and she could follow hers."

"I'm well aware of that, but we're together now, and I don't have any intention of letting her do it again."

"That's good to hear." He clears his throat, then states, "I just didn't want you to let her tenacity get in the way of something good for the two of you."

As I stare at him, it dawns on me. Now is as good a time as ever to check one of the most important things off my list that I had planned to do while she was away.

"Look, Herb, wait here. I've got something I want to show you."

Without waiting for him to respond, I rush to my room. Like a man on a mission, I quickly open my safe and pull out my purchase from DC.

When I return a few minutes later, Herb's in the same place I left him.

"I'm actually glad you stopped by, as it'll save me the trip," I muse, pulling out the box and setting it on the counter between us.

Now, it's his turn to be shocked and confused. Eyes wide, he asks, "What have you got there?"

"I want you to know without a doubt, Faye is it for me. I knew it mere days after seeing her again. I picked this up when I was in DC a few weeks ago. Go ahead," I say, shoving the box toward him. "Open it."

His jaw drops when his eyes land on the ring in front of him.

"She told you about my mother's earrings," he whispers in awe.

"Back when we were kids. But I remember," I assure him. "When the time is right, I intend to ask her to be my wife."

"I know it was rather presumptuous to show up like this, but you've always been straight with me. You've got too much of your mother in you not to. Our paths haven't crossed since the diner, and with Faye out of town, I'll admit... part of the reason I stopped by this afternoon is because I wanted to learn your intentions."

"I meant it when I said you're welcome anytime."

"Look, Mark, I'll be straight with you. I love my daughter to the ends of the earth. As you well know, she's strong and independent, and once she's made her mind up, there's nothing that will steer her from her course...." He inhales deeply, then shakes his head before adding, "That being said, I've also seen that she's quick to push everyone she loves away when things get stressful for her."

"I see some things haven't changed," I muse. "She'd do that when she was worked up about something while we were in school."

"The stakes get higher now that she's working for herself. For some damned reason, she always keeps the weight of the world on her shoulders alone and rarely lets anyone bear it with her."

"I'll keep that in mind," I assure him.

"I know you will. If anyone can get through to her, it's you. You were the only one who never let her close herself off and keep her burdens to herself." Then he chuckles. "I know it's not always easy, but I think you'll find your way with Faye."

He's got it all wrong. Faye does those things for me, as well. Instead of sharing that with him, though, I simply nod and say, "I appreciate the vote of confidence, Herb. It means a lot."

Not that I needed his approval, but now that I have it, a weight has been lifted.

Suddenly, Herb looks around my place. "Wow, you've certainly been busy with this place. I took a tour before it went on the market, and it looked nothing like this."

My chest puffs with pride as I look at my accomplishments through his eyes. "Yeah. This certainly has kept me busy since I bought it. I've still got plenty to do, but I'd be happy to show you around."

# Chapter 27
## Mark

"Hey, Dad. Can you grab that pool noodle?" Lanie asks the moment I walk into the indoor pool at Lizzy and Cameron's home.

"The green or the purple one?" I clarify, scooping them both off the concrete floor and walking toward the water.

"The purple one." Candace grins. "Vanny can have the green one."

Tossing the noodles toward each of the girls, I take a seat next to Lizzy on a lounge chair.

Settling back against the headrest, I slowly look around the active pool. As I watch my grandson dive and swim under the water as easily as he glides down the promenade on his skateboard, I can barely contain my excitement over how much improvement he's made. "Way to go, Jay!"

To Lizzy, I add, "One thing about Cameron purchasing this home is we've turned these kids into fish. Look at how much Jason alone has learned this summer."

"No kidding," Sloane muses from the other side of her. "Unlike last year, both Josh and Jason are begging to attend lessons each week because they want to beat the pants off Milli in the pool someday."

"Ah, the power of peer pressure." Lizzy chuckles. "Don't I know the blessing and the curse of it well."

"What curse?" Lanie scoffs, clearly not understanding.

"Said the oldest..." Raven deadpans. "Between you and Sloane, Liz and I never had a chance."

As I tune out my daughters' playful banter over the merits of peer pressure and birth order growing up, I focus on my grandkids playing in the pool. The kids are on their way to becoming great swimmers, but we always keep a sharp eye on them. With Lizzy's two youngest inside taking a nap and all four of my girls suited up to be in the pool should the need arise, I take this moment and settle further into my chair to do something I seldom do—relax.

Raven's girls, Vivy and Vanny, are so much like their mom and Sloane growing up, it's uncanny. I love their closeness. Somehow, their personalities are polar opposites, yet they always remain connected at the hip. My heart melts at the way their vibrant faces light up as they play with Milli and Candace in the shallow end of the pool, trying to synchronize their dance moves above and below the water. Ever since they all started gymnastics, we see their feet as much as their heads rise above the water at times like this.

The boys are zooming from the deep end to the middle, where they can touch. Carter's showing off, and Jason and Josh are eating up the new techniques he's teaching them from his lessons earlier this week.

These carefree afternoons are the things I missed so much when my girls were younger. As a dad, I was always in the thick of things. Between work and caring for the girls, there were many days I hardly knew which end was up. Since I shared visitation, I went out of my way to make every moment with them count when we were together.

*Gah, those were wild times.*

When I wasn't deployed or stationed abroad, I was always on the move and going to their next thing. I swear, there was never time to just be in the moment and simply exist. But this, right here, is what I love most about being a grandparent. Their parents get to do the hustle and bustle of everyday life, and I just get to tag along and enjoy the ride.

*I wonder what Faye would think of this beautiful chaos.*

Knowing her, she'd likely be in the pool and a part of the action, just like me.

If I hadn't just helped get the littles down for their naps, I'd already be waterlogged and zipping around the pool with the boys. I love the wild and crazy times as well as the calm ones with these kids.

Speaking of calm, I can't believe how sweet Everett was when I put him down for his nap. He reached up to cup my cheek and just stared into my eyes adorably for the longest time. Thinking he wanted to be tucked in tighter and given a good night kiss, like his mother usually does, I tried to kiss his cheek. But he just held my face and blinked, then whispered so his brother in the other room wouldn't hear, "Papa, can I come for a sleepover by my lonesome soon? Maybe we can play trucks and watch *Paw Patrol*."

Knowing Everett is a master of pulling at my heartstrings and trying to get me to talk, especially at nap time, I quickly told him I'd check with his mom. Then I promised we'd plan a Papa Date, as I like to call my one-on-one time with my grandkids.

I started these dates before my retirement. It not only gave each kid a break from their siblings, but it was the perfect opportunity for me to build close bonds with them. I watched my mother make a point of doing it with my girls, and it's something they cherish to this day. Now that I'm living in Seaside, it's much easier to plan dates with them around their busy schedules.

Speaking of dates, I wonder if Faye will reach out soon before she heads to bed.

*Gah, I can't believe it's been nearly three weeks since I've seen her in person.*

I miss her like crazy and find myself jumping every time my phone buzzes like a lost schoolboy, hoping like hell it's her. I know this is a great opportunity for her and her business, but selfishly, I hope this job ends soon, and she'll return to Seaside.

"Look at us, Papa," I hear from the other end of the pool.

Bringing my attention to the present, I proudly watch as all four of my granddaughters count out their performance, then twist, turn, and dive into the water in different directions, only to stand on their hands, then twist and come up for air. By the time they get to the end, they each pop up from the water at different times, and nothing about their well-practiced routine is remotely synchronized.

The moment their hands rise into the air to show their performance is finished, my hands are ready to fill the room with thunderous applause. Raven whistles, and their mothers cheer on their performance.

Once everything has settled, my mind returns to Faye for the millionth time today.

Reaching for my phone from the table beside me, I unlock it, then hesitate. Clearly, there are no notifications, but it doesn't mean I can't reach out and share this moment with her.

Opening my camera app, I quickly shoot a few pictures and a short video and send them to Faye, along with a message.

ME:

> Hey, sweetheart, thinking of you. Hope your meeting went well earlier.

I barely set my phone back on the table when it buzzes with an incoming text.

Within seconds, I've got my message app opened, and I find myself grinning at the beautiful face before me.

*Damn, she's stunning.*

FAYE:

> This is a selfie from my walk when I visited Suviana Lake instead of taking a lunch. I'm done for the day now and just got back to my hotel. I wish I were there, swimming with you. The kids look like they're having a blast.

For someone who's never had a family of her own, Faye's done remarkably well being around them. She never fails to ask about them and loves hearing the silly antics they get themselves into.

ME:

> You're welcome to join us anytime. After your meeting today, do you have an ETA for returning stateside?

FAYE:

> Unfortunately, I'm still waiting on a few parts. This hardware is really outdated and can't handle the bandwidth for the amount of data we need it to transfer.

My heart sinks when I read this. I'd really been hoping she'd finish it sooner than later, as she'd planned. I've never thought or cared about sufficient hard drives more than I have since she started this job.

FAYE:

On a positive note, I'm finally taking the weekend off. I'm thinking about traveling to Sienna and San Gimignano and just being a tourist.

ME:

That's great. You'll finally get a small break. You need it.

That's the understatement of the year. This woman puts me to shame when it comes to her work ethic. From sunrise to sunset and beyond, Faye grinds on for hours to complete her projects. I'm proud of her for taking some much-needed time for herself.

Just as I'm about to text her this, another text comes through.

FAYE:

Mom is calling. I'll call before heading to bed. XO

I'm not sure how long I stare at my phone, but suddenly, Lizzy shakes my arm to get my attention. "Dad, everything okay?"

"What?" I ask, looking around to ensure I haven't missed anything.

"Are you okay? You were smiling, then looked like you got some bad news."

"Faye has to stay in Italy for another week or two," I say before I can censor my thoughts.

"Is she working around the clock?" Lanie asks with interest.

"No," I huff out. "She's finally taking a break and doing some sightseeing this weekend. She must be at a standstill without the parts."

"You really like her, don't you?" Raven states, rather than asks, causing my head to whip in her direction.

"Would that be a problem if I did?" I sound more defensive than I intend.

Raven holds my gaze, then slowly grins. "No. I like her for you."

"We *all* do," Sloane chimes in. "But the question you have yet to fully address, *Colonel*... is... do you?"

"It isn't a matter of liking her," I admit.

"The hell it isn't." Raven smirks. "From the way I see it, you're beyond liking her."

Looking to each of my girls, I inhale deeply. "Yeah... I do."

"If you love her the way we think you do," Sloane chimes in, "then why aren't you with her?"

"That's a good question...." I muse more to myself than to her. "Wait, how do you know I love her?"

"Dad..." Raven shakes her head in annoyance. "It's insulting that you think you can hide things from us."

Well, if that isn't a kick in the pants. She's using one of my old phrases on me.

As I glance at each of my daughters, who stare expectantly at me, I realize there's no sense in denying it.

"Yeah. I love her... In fact, I'm fairly certain she's it for me."

"It?" Sloane's eyes nearly bulge out of their sockets in surprise.

"Yeah... *It* for me. As in, I'm hook, line, and sinker in love with Faye."

"So... I'm gonna repeat myself." Raven waits until my eyes meet hers before continuing. "What in the heck are you still doing in Seaside, then?"

"Uh, I live here?" I ask, completely confused by her question.

"Obviously." Lizzy rolls her eyes dramatically. "But what are you doing hanging out with us?"

"Uh... Now that I'm retired, I'm making up for lost time."

"Dad." Raven's disdain is clear. "I love you more than anything, but you're an idiot."

"Why? What did I do?"

"You should be with Faye," Lanie interjects.

"But she's working, and you all are here." I point out the obvious.

"Have you told Faye how you feel yet?" Lizzy asks.

"Uh... Not in so many words," I admit.

"Gah, you're such a guy," Raven guffaws. "We love you... you know that. But you should go be with Faye... and tell her how you feel."

"How? She's all the way in Italy. It's not like I can just walk over to her house to tell her," I point out.

Raven rolls her eyes and lets out a deep breath. "There's this little thing called a plane, maybe you've heard of it?"

Well, shit. She's got me there.

# Chapter 28
## Faye

As I wake up and roll over to check my phone, disappointment sets in that I haven't heard from Mark. On any other day, my schedule is packed so tight, I might not have noticed. But today, I have an entire weekend ahead of me with nothing concrete planned on my agenda. I've gotten used to my good morning texts or video calls from him.

I miss him like crazy and can't wait to get this job over with so I can go home.

Needing to hear his voice, I dial his number.

It goes straight to voicemail.

Hmmm. That's unusual. Perhaps he's just turned off his phone to sleep? I know he's been busting his ass working on projects around his house while the weather is good.

Suddenly, there's a knock at my door. "Room service."

That's funny. I didn't order anything.

*But sometimes, Mark does when he wants to ensure I've remembered to eat or treat me to something special.*

Smiling, I pull myself out of bed and grab my robe hanging by the closet.

By the time I get to the door, I've got it secured and knotted around my waist.

Outside my room, there's the expected food cart, along with the kind woman I've gotten to know over the last few weeks. "Good morning, Mira. How are you today?"

Mira's face lights up with a smile. "I'm doing well, thank you. Mr. Lancaster put an order in first thing this morning." There's a glint in her eyes, and she smiles. "He's a keeper, I tell you."

"Yeah." I nod in agreement. "He sure is."

*Gah, even from the other side of the world, this man regularly goes out of his way to show he's thinking of me. I'm not sure what I've done to deserve this, but I'll be forever grateful for the day Mark walked back into my life.*

When I finally pay attention to the cart between us, I see two plates instead of one. "What is this man up to?" I muse more to myself than to her.

Mira shrugs, then covers her mouth and uncharacteristically rushes to say, "Enjoy your day, Faye," before promptly turning to leave.

"Hmmm... That's odd," I mutter, then focus back on the food. Pulling off the lids, I see two orders of blueberry crêpes, bacon, and eggs. "Why on earth did Mark think I needed a double order?"

Out of nowhere, a familiar voice responds, "Perhaps he thought you'd want company for breakfast."

Instantly, my heart stops.

I swear I'm hearing things.

*Maybe I miss him so much, I'm hallucinating?*

When a tall figure from behind the wall moves into my direct line of sight, my breath catches in my throat. That is, until my brain finally registers—*Holy shit, it's really him!*

His handsome smile kickstarts my body into action, and

suddenly, I can't get to him fast enough. Fumbling with the cart, I attempt to push it out of the way, but it only runs into the doorjamb and gets stuck. I try again, and the wheel might as well be locked to the floor. Frustrated, I consider climbing over it.

Mark simply grins and effortlessly maneuvers it back into the hall.

The moment there's enough space, I squeeze past it and launch myself into his open arms.

"God, I've missed you," he murmurs as his strong, muscular arms wrap around me and squeeze me in the best way possible.

As I breathe in his masculine scent, I feel as if I've taken my first full breath of air since arriving in Italy. I had no idea just how much I've truly missed this man until this moment.

Pulling back to look him in the eye, I cup his face in my hands and laugh in disbelief. "Why didn't you tell me you were coming?"

"What would be the fun in that?" He smirks and squeezes my waist tighter.

Then, he lays a kiss on me that may as well burn the entire place down.

It's searing and all-consuming.

And entirely too short.

When he unfortunately breaks for air, he presses his forehead to mine and pants. "This... right here... was worth every second of sitting center seat in economy."

"You... You... sat center seat in economy?" I repeat, processing his words. Holy shit, it's at least a twelve-hour flight, and with his broad shoulders and long legs, that must've been miserable.

"Only for the last leg. That's what I get for booking a last-minute ticket. For the record, my favorite seat is in the cockpit, but beggars can't be choosers. I'm here and regret nothing."

When a door opens down the hall, Mark clears his throat and gives me one of his panty-melting smiles. "Mind if I join you for breakfast?"

"Only you would think to come all this way for breakfast," I tease, stepping back into the room.

Instantly, his eyes heat, and warmth courses through me. "Oh, trust me, Faye. I'm here for a whole lot more than that... But first..." He turns to grab the cart behind him. "Let's start with food. I'm starving."

Within minutes, we've got our plates set out in front of us at the conference table in my room. I'd booked a business suite out of necessity, knowing I'd be putting in long hours and needed a workspace conducive to getting this client on board. But now that I have company, I'm happy to have the additional space.

As we eat, he asks, "You still planning on touring Tuscany today?"

"I was... but I could be persuaded to do something else," I offer, glancing at the bedroom behind him.

Looking from the bedroom to me, he smirks mischievously. "Oh, sweetheart, there will be plenty of time for both. Trust me. But in all seriousness," he clears his throat, "mind if I join you in sightseeing? I know you need a break from this room *and,* more than anything, a break from your project. You've been working around the clock and deserve a few days off."

He quirks a brow, as if he's waiting for me to protest.

When I don't say anything, he adds, "I only have one request..."

"What's that?"

"That we start with a shower. I've been traveling for over a day, and I want to freshen up before I get *you* dirty."

# Chapter 29
## Mark

The heat in Faye's eyes has me hoping she'll join me in the shower.

As much as I'd love that shower to start now, I see she's barely touched her food, and I have plans for us today. Picking up a piece of my own bacon, I point to her plate. "Eat, sweetheart. We've got the whole day ahead of us."

"Hmmm... The whole day..." she draws out, picking up a piece of bacon for herself and pointing it in my direction. "Just how long are you stayin', Lancaster?"

"Depends..." I muse, mimicking her quizzical expression.

"On?" she probes adorably.

Plastering a stoic expression, I fight like hell to keep from cracking as I state, "On when you can get this client up and running."

"Mark..." she gasps, disbelief written all over her face. "I-I have no idea how much longer this will take. It could be another couple of weeks."

Shrugging, I take a bite of my bacon and chew. "It's a good thing I'm due for a vacation, then. Apparently..." I feel my face finally break, and I'm certain a smug grin forms when I add, "That's what one does when they retire."

"But what about your kids? Are you sure you want to be away from them that long?"

The fact that they're included in her list of worries proves she gets me.

A low laugh escapes as I admit, "They're the ones who gave me the much-needed kick in the pants to get my ass here in the first place. Besides, it's only a few weeks. They'll survive without me."

"Are you sure?"

"As long as I'm back for the festival, I'm good. Apparently, there are these tin cans that fly in the sky called planes. Who knew?"

Shoving my shoulder, she chortles. "Gah, you're such a smartass."

"Well, that's the argument that got me here in the first place, so you can thank them for pointing out that little tidbit."

Adorably, she rolls her eyes and laughs. "Are you serious?"

"I wasn't exactly subtle in keeping my feelings about you to myself, Faye. They saw right through my BS and called me on it."

Faye attempts but miserably fails at keeping the smile from her face. "That would've been a sight worth seeing."

"Let's just say, they got the drop on me and had my number before I could even clock it."

Leaning in, she kisses my cheek. "Well, I, for one, am grateful to them. I've missed you like crazy."

"Same, sweetheart. Same."

Suddenly, the hotel phone rings, scaring the shit out of both of us.

Rushing to the phone, she answers, "Hello?"

Someone says something on the other line, and Faye

hurries to her nightstand to pick up her cell phone. "Oh... Sorry, Mom. I must've had my phone on vibrate."

"How are you?" she asks, sitting on the edge of the bed.

From the other room, she covers the phone and mouths, "*Sorry.*"

"No problem," I whisper and go back to finishing my breakfast.

*Damn, these crêpes are amazing.*

As I eat, I do my best to give them their privacy, but the hotel suite is only so big.

From what I can gather, her mom fills her in about her father's latest venture to the hardware store and how well her strawberries are growing. Faye barely gets a word in edgewise as her mom prattles from one subject to the next.

When I finish eating, I lean against the doorway and thumb toward the bathroom. "Mind if I shower?"

She purses her lips, then nods slowly and mouths, "*Go ahead.*"

I barely have shampoo in my hair when I hear the click of the bathroom door. Slowing my regular routine, I take my time to lather the soap through my hair. I hear the toilet flush, then water from the sink turns on as I rinse off.

Now that my shampoo has been rinsed, I watch her dry her hands and brush her teeth. My cock bobs to life when she disrobes and steps into the shower with me.

"Fuck, you're beautiful, Faye," I practically growl, reaching for her.

"You're not so bad yourself, Lancaster. I thought I could slow down your shower routine a bit and perhaps join you?"

"Like you *ever* need an invitation."

"I don't know, Mark... I'm rather fond of long showers..." she draws out playfully as she runs her hand down my abdomen. "I wouldn't want to feel rushed."

My muscles flex involuntarily, and I fight the urge to bend her against the wall and have my way with her. "I know how to take my time when it matters, Faye."

Bracing my hand against the wall behind her, I cup her ass and squeeze with the other, as she fists my growing cock. "Hmm... Someone's happy to see me."

"He ain't the only one," I promise as I crash my lips to hers.

She tastes of mint and carnal need as she opens herself to me. I've missed her so much, and I truly can't get enough. As much as I want to take things slow and sweet, it's been way too long.

Sure, we've gotten each other off on the phone over the last few weeks. But now that I'm here in person, I want to make good on all those late-night promises I've made. I distinctly recall her saying she likes it when I suck on her nipples as I slide my fingers through her folds.

So, I do just that. Over and over until she's writhing with need.

"Mmmm... Mark... That feels good," Faye murmurs as she clings to me.

"Even in the shower, I can feel you're soaked for me, sweetheart."

Needing more, I flip us around so she's the one under the streaming water.

When I feel her tremble, I drop to my knees and prop one of her thighs on my shoulder.

Her hands grasp me tight as she finds her balance.

The moment I slide my tongue where my fingers had been, moans of pleasure fill the room, and her hands fist my hair tightly.

My dick turns to stone as she gasps, "Oh, God... That feels... Ohmigod... Right there..." She arches her sweet pussy forward, giving me even better access.

Lapping from her center to her tight bud, I slide two fingers deep inside her.

Her walls tighten, and she clamps down around my fingers like a vise. When I find that squishy spot along her front wall that drives her wild, she groans out my name. Keeping a steady massaging rhythm, I suck her clit into my mouth and flick my tongue against her as quickly and hard as I can.

A slew of curses spews from her mouth as she fists my hair and presses me harder against her. "Ohmigod... Mark... I'm..."

That's all the warning I get before her body stiffens and her walls quake violently from within. I stay right with her, pulse after pulse, until her body goes slack.

Slowly, I help her lower her leg and stand to face her. "You doin' okay?" I grin triumphantly, brushing the wet hair from her face.

"Better than okay... That was... Ohmigod... I have no words," she whispers blissfully, with the most beautiful smile stretched across her features.

Leaning in, I kiss her.

As she kisses me back, I'm suddenly keenly aware that shower sex won't cut it. I need to ravage every inch of her body, and a bed would be much better suited for what I have in mind.

"Let's wash you up and get out of here," I offer when her body slinks against mine for support.

She simply nods and lets me care for her completely.

By the time we get out of the shower and dry off, we're making out like crazy on the way to the bedroom. When she scrambles to the center of the bed, and I start to crawl on top of her, a wicked thought hits.

Arching a brow in challenge, I ask, "Where do you keep your vibrator?"

"Mark..." she chastises as she reaches for me. "I just want you."

"You'll get me," I promise. "But you've been teasing me off and on for weeks, and now that I'm here in person, I want a chance to play with you, like I've promised."

For the first time in forever, Faye's beautiful body blushes from head to toe. "I-It's... in the nightstand," she stammers.

Reaching over, I pull open the drawer but don't see anything but a small fabric bag. Pulling it out, I hold it up for her to see. "In here?"

When Faye nods, I feel like the Cheshire cat as all our conversations play back on a loop through my mind. "Hmmm... Where to start?" I ask, pulling the light-purple vibrator out of the bag.

When a small, round object falls out along with it, I look to Faye for further explanation.

Her heated eyes meet mine, and she licks her lower lip with her tongue. Breathlessly, she admits, "It's a remote."

"Oh... Fuck me... We're gonna have some fun with this," I promise as I take a few minutes to figure out how it works. Not only does it straighten into a wand with a button you can turn on from the vibrator itself, but it also completely cups into the shape of a C. After pressing the button a few times, I quickly find there are three distinct speeds and several rhythmic patterns.

"You have a favorite?" I ask, wanting to ensure she gets the most pleasure out of this.

"It varies, depending on my mood," she admits, propping herself onto her elbows to watch me.

"Hmm... So many possibilities. You mentioned something about this being the perfect toy for flying solo or with a couple?"

"I've only used it solo," she promises. "But I've always wanted to try it with a partner."

Reaching for it, she cups it into a C and says, "When this is inserted like this, it simultaneously presses against my clit and g-spot. Apparently, there's enough room that you can slide behind it, and we'll both enjoy it."

"What about the remote?" I ask, lying beside her and tracing my fingers along her inner thighs. The way she squirms in anticipation has me dying to experience this with her.

"It... can be in your hand or mine."

Pressing it into her palm, I lean in to kiss her lips tenderly. Then I admit, "I've never been inside someone with a toy like this... Why don't you surprise us both with whatever you're in the mood for."

Pulling my face to hers, she kisses me. "I can't believe I get another of your firsts," she teases.

Running a finger through her folds, I grin and promise, "I want the rest of my firsts with you, Faye." Turning on the vibrator, I trace the movement of my fingers. "Show me how you want it, sweetheart."

With a wicked grin on her lips, she confidently takes the vibrator from my hands, bends it into the correct position, then rubs it against herself until it is completely inserted. Switching the vibration to the lowest speed, she warns, "I need this slow if you're gonna be inside me, too."

Shifting so I hover over her, I grip my cock and tug it twice, trying to release some of my tension. Faye's eyes heat, and she moans as she scooches down the bed further. "Let me lick you first, Mark. That was hot."

As she reaches for my cock, I sit up on my knees to give her access. As her tongue glides from the base to my tip, I growl. "Fuck..." Then warn, "If you want me inside of you, you need to stop."

"I'm already so close," she moans, lying back on the bed. "I wanna feel you come inside me, Mark."

In a matter of seconds, I'm lined up and pressing against

the vibrator. "Not sure how long I'll last," I warn. Then ask, "Mind if we turn this off until I get inside?"

I need to make sure she likes this before taking it to the next level.

Her warmth and slickness are beyond measure as I slip inside her tightness. "Fuck," I groan when I'm fully seated inside her.

"God... This feels so good," she pants, as we find a rhythm between us.

Just when we hit our stride, there's a light buzzing sensation against my shaft. "Holy... Fuckin' Christ..." I grunt as I falter at first, but then push through to regain our rhythm.

It doesn't take long before I hear the telltale signs of Faye's impending orgasm.

"This is hot as fuck! You're so beautiful, Faye," I say as we pick up our pace.

Couple that with the way she stiffens, and suddenly, I'm dying to chase that orgasm right along with her. When she clings to me tightly, I feel her inner walls grip me like I've never been gripped in my life, and my orgasm barrels through me like a runaway freight train, completely out of control.

Pressing into her, my entire body rocks as pulse after pulse of energy rips through me. Holding her tight, I release everything I have into her. I've never come so hard in my entire life, and with the cramped space inside her, everything is intensified beyond measure.

Eventually, the vibrating between us stops. All I can do is lie there on top of her. I prop myself onto my elbows to keep from crushing her and try to catch my breath.

When I'm finally able to lift my head and look her in the eye, a lazy grin spreads across her beautiful face. Love radiates through her, along with a bewildered expression.

Leaning down, I kiss her lightly. "I love you, Faye.

"I love you, too, Mark," she whispers, then shakes her head and giggles, rocking our sensitive bodies. "Holy fucking shit, Mark... That was one of the hottest and most intense orgasms of my life."

"Right there with you, sweetheart," I agree and kiss her once again.

# Chapter 30
## Faye

Three hours later, Mark and I are finally ready to leave. We've decided to drive to San Gimignano first, and if we have time, we'll visit Sienna, too. Not that I'm complaining about our late start, but we agree to take a change of clothes in case we decide to stay somewhere along the way, rather than drive the few hours back to Bologna.

While I get ready after our second shower of the morning, Mark takes the liberty of packing our things for the trip. He'd somehow gone to the market and grabbed a few items for our road trip in that short time, as well.

To my surprise, he rented a fancy Mercedes that's roomy and super comfortable to ride in. The sleek car grips the corners of the scenic highway and makes for an incredible experience.

From the moment we hit the open road, his hand grips mine as it rests on my lap. Like everything with Mark, our playful banter helps pass the time with ease. Low music plays in the background as he catches me up on each of his daughters and their families, and I fill him in on my conversation with Mom from this morning.

Once we turn off the main highway in Poggibonsi, I'm in awe as we ascend the Tuscan hills. "Mark..." I sigh heavily. "These olive groves and vineyards are breathtaking. I've visited Italy countless times but have never taken the time to just relax and enjoy it all, ya know."

"That's the point, Faye." He shrugs. "You need a break."

"I know." I sigh heavily, forcing myself further into the seat. "I know better, but it's easier said than done to truly make myself stop."

"For the record, I'm just as guilty of never relaxing. I've been so used to being on the go, I hardly know what to do with myself when I get free time."

"Aren't we a pair," I muse.

"Oh, look," I gasp. I think we're almost there." I point to the medieval towers in the distance."

"Would you be up for having a picnic before we explore the city itself? I had the hotel pack us lunch for when we were ready. I've got it in a cooler in the trunk. There's supposed to be a scenic view just up ahead."

"You're rarely unprepared, huh, Lancaster?" I tease. I swear, in a prior life, he must have been a Boy Scout. I guess that's what being in the Air Force for thirty years has done to him.

As much as I'd love to explore the quaint little town behind the brick walls, I know I'd enjoy it more on a full stomach. "That sounds amazing. What's for lunch?"

Mark's low chuckle fills the car. "Your guess is as good as mine. I asked them to pack us something fitting for this trip. Mira put in my order and placed it in a cooler for safekeeping."

When a spot along the narrow road widens, Mark pulls off and parks. He walks around and opens my door, then goes to the trunk. To my surprise, he's brought a blanket. Unfolding the blanket, he spreads it over a patch of grass with the perfect view of the medieval-like city, then gestures for me to sit.

Taking off my sandals, I take a seat on the blanket.

After Mark does the same, he rummages in the small chest. First, he brings out two plates, then a larger container. When he takes off the lid, I'm surprised to find a charcuterie platter filled with a variety of meats, cheeses, olives, and two different types of bread. Off to the side, there are fresh grapes, sliced peaches, cherries, dried apricots, and a variety of nuts.

"I know you enjoy sparkling wine, so they've also packed us a local prosecco." Mark holds out the bottle with a corkscrew, and I nod happily.

"Mmm... This all looks delicious," I admit. "I'd love a glass of wine."

"Help yourself to food," he offers as he pours us each a glass.

Once he hands me mine, he settles on the blanket beside me.

"Ahhh, this is delicious." I exhale heavily after taking a sip. The wine tastes fruity, yet crisp, with a hint of pear.

"I'm so glad you're here to share this with me," I admit. "I truly don't think I would've actually stopped to just enjoy the view like this if you weren't here."

"I meant it when I said I want to experience everything with you, Faye." Mark shrugs. "I love you, and I can't imagine spending any more time apart from you."

"I feel the same. For the first time since I can remember, this trip has been much harder on me than I care to admit. I'm fairly certain you're to blame for that, Lancaster," I tease, then give him a playful shove to lighten the mood. "It's like you made me fall for you all over again."

His voice is rough as he admits, "As a perpetual bachelor,

I'm not used to feeling tethered to anyone. Yet, when you aren't with me, I feel like I'm going out of my mind. For the record, you're the only one who's ever impacted me like this." Mark reaches for my hand and squeezes it before continuing. "From the second I saw you again, I haven't stopped thinking of you."

"It's funny, I thought my feelings for you had long disappeared, but the moment you waltzed back into my life, they were back with a vengeance," I confess in return.

"I'm not sure I've ever stopped loving you, Faye," Mark admits, brushing a loose strand of hair from my face.

With his eyes locked on mine, my voice hitches as I admit, "Me neither."

Mark sets his glass of wine on the chest in front of us, then pops onto his knees to face me. Predatorily, he crawls toward me with a wicked gleam in his eyes. "Well, Faye Julianna Ames..." He stops and sits back on his haunches. "I guess there's only one thing you can do about it then..."

Placing my glass beside me on the grass, I get on my knees to meet his challenge. "What's that, Lancaster?"

A sexy, smug smirk fills his face. "You'll just have to agree to spend forever with me."

"Is that right?"

I playfully tease, though my heart is zipping a million miles a minute, declaring my love for him like this.

"Yep. But this time... we make it official," he declares as if it makes all the sense in the world.

"Official? What the hell are you talking about?" I attempt to process his words.

Reaching behind the cooler, he grabs something, then scooches onto one knee to get closer to me, with a challenge in his eye as he states, "I've loved you since I was a young and dumb teenager and let you go. I'm more in love with you now than I could ever imagine. Faye Julianna Ames, will you put me out of my misery and agree to be my wife?"

"Wha—" I start, but Mark reaches for my hand and cuts me off.

When his eyes lock on mine, I feel his question deep in my soul.

"Will you marry me, Faye?"

Tears prick my eyes, and a state of shock consumes me. I barely notice him flipping the box open or the ring inside. All I can do is nod profusely and throw myself at him.

The moment our lips touch, I kiss him like I've never kissed anyone before. His love pours through me, and I truly can't get enough.

When a car approaches, we break apart, panting.

With a knowing grin, he clarifies, "Is that a yes?"

"Yes, you fool. It's a yes. I'll marry you!"

"Whew..." He pretends to wipe sweat from his brow, then pulls me in for a hug. "Let's put this ring on you and take a selfie so we can send it to my kids."

I finally notice the ring itself, and I start crying all over again.

Holy shit, this man has a bigger memory capacity than most of the software I develop. I swear, it's like he knows me better than I know myself.

In awe, I wonder, "How on earth did you take a window-shopping experience from nearly thirty years ago and make it become our reality?"

"Easy, sweetheart." He squeezes me tight from the side as we focus on the ring. "I pay attention."

As he slips the ring onto my finger, I can't stop staring at its utter perfection.

The vintage white-gold band fits perfectly on my finger. There's a square blue sapphire set in the center that would match my grandmother's earrings perfectly, with two smaller diamonds flanking each side.

With his arm around my waist, Mark leans in and says, "The color should be a perfect match to go with your grandmother's earrings. But that's not the only reason I picked this particular ring, though. This style is perfect for us. Not only is it vintage, in that it will stand the test of time, but, Faye, you need to know... You are my one true love from my past. The one I can't live without in my present, and the only one I ever want to love in my future."

My heart can't contain how happy I am in this moment.

"Ohmigod, Mark," I gush, cupping his cheek. "I love you."

"I love you more, sweetheart," Mark whispers.

"Did you know that day I told you about my grandmother's earrings, I'd wished for a ring just like this from you?"

"I may not have been ready then, but I won't make that mistake twice. I can't wait to spend the rest of forever with you, sweetheart."

Pulling me in for another searing kiss, I let my love for him shine through. He's the only man I've ever loved, and I can't wait to see what our future holds.

As another car breaks us apart, Mark grins wildly and suggests, "Now, about that selfie?"

"Wait... Your kids knew you were going to propose?"

"Nope... But this should have the family group chat going off like a firecracker for the foreseeable future. Just wait until you get added."

# Chapter 31
## Lancaster's Group Chat

MARK:

Just checking in…

MARK:

(Image of Faye and Mark in Tuscany—her ring on full display)

MARK:

She said YES!

*(Faye has been added to the chat.)*

JAX:

Whoa… hold on… rushing to get Sloane. (sprinting emoji)

JAX:

Congrats, BTW—but this is HUGE! (mind blown emoji)

LANIE:

WHAT?!?!?!? OMG! Congrats.

LIZZY:

Seriously? Wow! Love you both.

RAVEN:

And you all say I'm the wild card?

LIZZY:

We all knew Dad was in love with Faye...
You're still the wild card, Raven.

RAVEN:

BTW, congrats, Dad and Faye.

RYAN:

Whew... the cat's finally out of the bag. I've
been waiting for this to finally be dropped.
FYI, Mr. Ames has loose lips and has been
hoping this happens soon. Congratulations!
I'm happy for the two of you.

JAX:

Dad mentioned this could be a possibility—
I've been fielding questions from my mom for
at least a week or so. I had no idea how to
answer.

SLOANE:

Seriously? Jax and Ryan knew about this
first? I'm highly offended.

RYAN:

Get up early and go to coffee at the diner,
then you'll always be in the know. It's where I
get all the news in this town.

CAMERON:

Dude. You do realize how old you sound
right? Hanging out with the town biddies
waiting on gossip?

CAMERON:

Congrats Mark and Faye!

RYAN:

You're still WAAAY older than me, Cam.

FINN:

Congratulations, Colonel. I'm happy for you.

FAYE:

Thanks for the well-wishes.

MARK:

Faye and I are off to San Gimignano. We're turning off our phones so you can blow each other's phones up for the foreseeable future. Glad we've given you something to talk about. (winking emoji)

LANIE:

Love you, Dad! Have fun. Faye, I can't wait to hear all about it.

LIZZY:

Same. Love you both!

RAVEN:

Way to keep us on our toes! Love you!

SLOANE:

Love you. Have fun, be safe... and don't do anything we wouldn't do!

FINN:

It's like you've just given him permission to run off and have sex. (plugs ears and runs away... lalalalala)

JAX:

Okay... I'm out.

RYAN:

Me too.

RAVEN:

But it was just getting fun. I love it when Finn blushes.

LANIE:

Okay... gotta run!

# Chapter 32
## Faye

Mark wasn't kidding when he said he wanted to spend forever with me, starting as soon as possible. We no sooner get back to the States, and he asks me about dates. Knowing all of his family and mine would be in town for the Seaside Music Festival, we decided to ask them to stay a couple more days and get married the Tuesday after the chaos of the festival is over.

I'm quickly learning that if you need anything done in this family, Sloane makes it happen. All the girls will pitch in at a moment's notice, but she's the one who has an uncanny ability to really put things into action. Within days of asking, she has helped secure nearly everything we need—except for my dress.

When Mark hears his girls and me talking about the issue, he makes it possible for them to join my mom and me in Portland to look at dresses. Knowing I want to spend more time with his daughters, he personally watches all nine of his grandkids while we make the trip. We have the best time laughing, sipping champagne, and telling stories about Mark. He pretends to grumble about it, but we all know he loves that his daughters and I are becoming fast friends. The best part is, I came home with a dress that day, and it's perfect for me.

*The big day is finally here.*

I'm officially marrying the only man I've ever truly loved.

There's only one place our wedding could be held: where it all began, at Mark's childhood home.

As I put my finishing touches on my makeup in Lanie's bedroom, I hear a knock at the door.

Mom steps in and gasps. "Oh, Faye. You're just... breathtaking."

"Thanks, Mom," I say, standing to hug her.

"Being back in this house makes me miss Jane something fierce. She and I always wished the two of you would run into one another. We just *knew* the sparks would fly because you two always had the strongest chemistry. We knew it even before you did as teens."

"Really?" I ask in disbelief. "Why didn't you ever tell me? I spent years avoiding Mark, only to fall in love with him the second I saw him again."

"Oh," she tsks and swats a hand in the air. "Jane and I never wanted to meddle. We'd hoped you'd find your way back to each other but didn't want to sway your destiny. I have something I'd like you to read, though, to prove I'm not pulling your leg about this."

Placing my hand on hers, I assure her, "Mom, I trust you."

Taking a long breath, Mom smiles and digs into her purse. "Jane would've wanted you to read this, as well. She and I used to write one another when she'd travel with the girls to visit Mark. This is one of the last letters she ever sent me."

My heart thunders in my chest as she hands me the envelope.

As I open it, my chest squeezes when I immediately recognize Jane Lancaster's familiar cursive script.

Dear Virgie,

I hope this letter finds you well. I am loving each and every moment with my granddaughters this summer, but I miss home all the same. There's something to be said about waking up next to the ocean each morning. I don't sleep as well without it lulling me to sleep, but we're both at that fantastic age where sleep evades us, so it doesn't really matter, does it?

The girls and I are heading to London in the morning. With Lanie starting college and the rest officially in high school, it might be one of the last family trips they're all obligated to partake in. I know they don't really need me, but with Mark only getting leave for the second half of our trip, I promised I'd spend the entire two weeks taking them to sites around the UK before he arrives. So, they're eager for our adventure together.

Speaking of Mark, I love my son to the ends of the earth and back, but sometimes I want to rip his arms off and beat him with them. He's a phenomenal father and has had an outstanding career, but he needs to learn there's more to life than that. He and I were talking about home last night, and somehow the subject of Faye came up.

I'm not saying this to bring either of us false hope, but you should've seen the way his eyes lit up when he talked about her. Even after all these years, I sometimes wonder if she'll be the only person he ever truly loves.

Oh, don't get me wrong. He loved Sarah in his own way. She gave him four amazing children, and he repeatedly says he has zero regrets about how things started or ended with them. But even after all these years, I've never seen him light up the way he does when he talks about Faye.

I also know our sweet Faye avoids poor Mark like the plague. But even you have to admit... there's something to be said about <u>never</u> talking about someone. The last time she came to visit, I caught her staring at a picture of him with an expression much like his when he talked about her yesterday. She loves hearing all the stories she can about his girls, but clams up when I start talking too much about Mark himself. So, of course, I do my best to sprinkle in details every now and then, to let her know he's still single.

I'm not sure what her hang-up is over Mark, but I hope I get to see her resolve those feelings in my lifetime. Mark my words (no pun intended), if those two ever sit in the same room again, I'm certain they'll be right back to where they started in no time.

She's worked hard over the years, and she, too, has a phenomenal career, but you and I both know she's also kept her heart guarded. Even if it's not with Mark, I hope she truly finds a way to bring love into her life. She is far too special a person to spend her life alone. She has so much love in her, and I hope she gets to share it with someone special.

I know I sound like a ridiculous busybody, but you of all people know how strong my intuition can be. I had to take a moment and write it down, or no one would ever believe me should this finally happen in the future.

Of course, I won't do anything to interfere with their fate, but between you and me, this is something I feel deep in my bones will happen. The two of them just need to pull their heads out of their stubborn asses and simply be in the same room with one another to let it happen.

Until then, I'll just mind my business, and you be sure to do the same.

Please send Herb my love. If you have a chance, feel free to stop by my garden and pick anything you'd like for yourself. I'd hate for any of it to go to waste while I'm galavanting through the British countryside.

Take care. I miss you tons, but I'm loving every moment with my girls and wouldn't miss this time with them for the world.

Until next time,

Jane

·  ·  ·

BY THE TIME I get to the end, tears stream down my face. "Oh, Mom." I gush, throwing myself into her arms and squeezing her tight.

When I pull back, I suck in a deep breath and admit, "I've been missing Jane so much today."

"She's always here, sweetheart. She loved you so much."

"Can I get a copy of this letter to share with Mark? I'm sure he's missing his mom like crazy on a day like today."

"Oh, Faye," she sighs. "You can have it. I think this is something you should share with Mark when you feel the time is right."

When I spot my reflection in the mirror, I laugh. "It's a good thing I'm wearing waterproof makeup, or I'd be starting from ground zero again." Taking a tissue, I dab at my eyes and grin excitedly. "Can you send Dad in here? I think I'm ready to officially start my forever with Mark."

# Epilogue
## Mark

Standing here at the altar, with all my friends and family beside me, as I wait for the love of my life to join me, is one of the best feelings in the world. It may have been more than thirty years in the making, but today, Faye officially becomes my wife.

Knowing Jax and Finn would be busy with their families today, Ryker, the only member of Ruby Frax who isn't part of my immediate family, volunteered to play his guitar for the prelude of our ceremony. As his upbeat melody mixes with the wind on the beach, I anxiously wait for my bride to make her entrance.

"You doin' okay over there, Lancaster?" Enzo, my best man, quietly asks, nudging my shoulder. "Remember to unlock your knees, or I'm gonna end up having to save your ass."

Shifting my weight, I grin at his attempt at humor. "I'm good, Harps." After thirty years in the Air Force, he knows damn well I could stand at attention until the cows come home without my knees locking.

Enzo Harper never in a million years thought that being my best man would be the way he returned the favor owed to me.

You should've seen the expression on his face the day I went to collect—it was priceless. I know he would have done it regardless, but I'm sure I'll never hear the end of it either. He never thought that I, Mark Lancaster, the eternal bachelor, had finally fallen head-over-heels in love. He graciously accepted two weeks ago and couldn't wait to see the woman who had brought me to my knees.

I'm thrilled he and Samantha, as well as their two younger children, could take time out of their busy schedules to be a part of our wedding. Last night at the rehearsal dinner, Faye and his wife, Sam, got along well. I can tell they're on the fast track to being close friends.

An excited energy courses through me as Faye's brother escorts his mother to her seat. Once everyone is settled, Ryker takes his cue and changes the tune to "Pachelbel's Canon in D Major."

Slowly, Faye's sister, Carolyn, walks down the short aisle between the white chairs we've set out on the beach. My heart races when the song gets louder, and the notes shift to signal Faye's arrival.

She's remained hidden behind the tiny dunes between the house and where we're getting married. My breath catches when she finally comes into view. Not only do her eyes shine with love I can feel deep in my soul, but her smile radiates and fills me with a need I can barely contain.

My body itches to close the distance between us, and I almost say *fuck it* and go to her, but Enzo taps my arm and whispers, "Easy now. Let her have her moment to shine."

That's all it takes to keep me rooted in place.

I marvel at her beauty as she makes her way to me.

From the way her hair is contained in a whimsical updo, to the fitted bodice with the most intricate lace that drops to a shimmery full-length A-line skirt that billows in the wind as she walks, Faye is utter perfection.

When Faye stops before me, and the officiant finally starts the ceremony, my mind is entirely lost on her. As I marvel in her beauty, I'm vaguely aware of her dad giving his blessing and taking his seat.

The moment Faye reaches for me and clasps her hands in mine, all is right in my world.

Thankfully, Faye and I agreed to keep our ceremony short. If I were given a quiz on what was said specifically, I'd fail miserably. But I can tell you the exact color of her eyes in this light, the number of strands in her beautiful blonde hair that lose their fight to the wind, and the way Faye's laugh lines form a second before her lips turn into the most breathtaking smile.

When it comes time for the vows, I force myself to focus.

Squeezing her hand, I clear my throat and project so everyone can hear. "Faye, I'm not sure I remember the exact day we became friends, but I'm certain I can tell you the exact moment I considered you as more."

The small crowd gathered roars in laughter, so I'm forced to wait for them to settle before continuing.

"It was the summer between our sophomore and junior year. We were connected at the hip most days, and you went from being my best friend to being the only woman in the world for me. I distinctly remember thinking as I looked into your gorgeous blue eyes as we sat here on this very beach, *Holy shit. I love this girl.*"

This earns more laughter from our friends and family.

"Mark." She shakes her head and bats at my shoulder.

"You were smart, funny, and the most beautiful woman in the world. You pushed me and challenged me to become the man I am today... Even if it meant taking a thirty-year pause," I add in for good measure.

"Now that I'm back, you won't be able to shake me so easily, sweetheart."

Her beautiful laugh fills the space between us.

When she settles, I go in for the kill.

"Faye, I promise to love, honor, and cherish you for the rest of my life. I guarantee there will be times that I'm stubborn, tenacious ... and let's face it... just an outright idiot."

My family laughs, but I keep pushing through.

"We may not always see eye to eye, but I vow, right here in front of... well, everyone... the decisions I make will be with both of our interests in mind. I promise to show up, support you, and be there for you in ways no man ever has. Your heart is precious, and I promise to treat it with kindness, respect, and most of all... love."

The officiant says something to Faye, but my only concern is her words to me.

"Mark... You have always been a force to be reckoned with. You're strong, loyal, and you love with your whole heart. You see things from perspectives I may not... But that doesn't mean you don't share the same goals."

Taking a breath, she pushes some loose hair from her face before continuing. "I fell in love with you long before I ever admitted it. For as long as I can remember, you were the standard I held all others to. Fortunately for you," she says pointedly, "no other measured up."

The crowd erupts with laughter, knowing damn well she's made a good point.

"Thank God for that," someone in the audience hollers, but I don't care to know who. The second Faye squeezes my hand, my entire focus returns to her.

Tears prick my eyes when her sincerity rings through. "Mark, I promise to love, honor, and cherish you. I promise to make goals *with* you and share my life with you. Most of all, I promise to never stop loving you the way you deserve."

The next few minutes are a blur of exchanging our rings.

Finally, the most important phrase is uttered, "I now pronounce you husband and wife. Mark, you may kiss your bride!"

I don't hesitate.

Cupping my hand to her cheek, I lean in and kiss her.

The moment our lips touch, her fist clenches my shirt, and she pulls me closer.

Her lips part with ease, and it takes everything in me not to completely lose myself in us. When the thunderous applause erupts, hoots, hollers, and loud, boisterous whistles join in.

Eventually, we take the hint and break apart.

As my eyes lock on hers, I run my thumb along her lower lip as I whisper, "I'm not even close to being done with you, sweetheart." Then I tilt my head in the direction of our audience. "I do believe we have a reception to attend."

The heat in her eyes makes sparks flash up my spine.

With a playful grin, she says, "What do ya say, Landcaster? You ready to show me a good time on that dance floor those boys built?"

"Sweetheart, I'm always up for a good time. But you should know, I'm here for a long time. I want forever with you, Faye."

Taking her hand in mine, I lead her down the aisle.

As each of our friends and family shouts well-wishes as we pass, a thought hits me right in the chest. Looking around at everyone who came to celebrate this occasion with us, it's hard to imagine what we've been through to get here.

For two people who couldn't wait to leave this town all those years ago, I'm certainly glad we both came back to call Seaside our home. I can't imagine my life without my family, and most importantly, my beautiful wife, Faye.

. . .

## THE END

I HOPE you've enjoyed reading Mark and Faye's story in The *Summer I Found Home*. This story marks the end of an era for me as an author, as it is the end of *The Summers in Seaside* series. If you're new to me, and you've fallen in love with many of the people in this story, you'll be happy to know this likely won't be the last time you hear about these characters. I write primarily in one world and love nothing more than to connect my stories with crossovers.

IF YOU WANT to find out Mark's reaction to his mother's letter, please **click here for exclusive bonus content**. **Or you can visit** https://geni.us/ASBCTSIFH to grab a copy for yourself today.

AUTHOR'S NOTE: **If you like reading books set in one world, you'll be happy to find several full-length stories for several of the characters mentioned in *The Summer I Found Home* already written and available on my website www.amandashelley.com.**

ENZO HARPER'S story is featured in *The Resilience Duet*. Find out how this elite rescue pilot, home on leave, meets his match with a single mom with no filter. Check out their story today: https://geni.us/B2RResilience

RYAN AND LANIE'S story began in *The Summer Dare*. This Summer Love/Falling for Contractor romance is available to start reading today. https://books2read.com/SummerDare

Sloane and Jax's story is featured in *The Summer Ultimatum*. You can grab your copy of this rockstar romance today and start reading: https://books2read.com/SummerUltimatum

RAVEN AND FINN'S story is featured in *The Summer Proposal*. This is a case of mistaken identity and fake-dating a rockstar. You can grab their story today: https://books2read.com/SummerProposal

LIZZY AND CAMERON'S story is featured in *The Summer Arrangement*. It is a second-chance, single-dad-falling-for-the-nanny romance. Start reading their story today: https://books2read.com/TheSummerArangement

# ACKNOWLEDGMENTS

First, I would like to thank you the reader, blogger, and reviewer for taking the time to read this book. There are so many stories to choose from, and I'm humbly honored you've chosen to read mine. I hope you enjoyed Mark and Faye's story. If you want more from the from their word, be sure to check out the Summers in Seaside Series.

I'd love to hear from you and your thoughts about Mark and Faye. You can find me on social media, my reader's group *Amanda's Army of Readers*, or at www.amandashelley.com. If you care to share your thoughts on this book with other book lovers, please consider leaving a review at any of the retail sites or on Goodreads, BingeBooks, and BookBub.

I'd like to thank C.L. Collier for being my partner in crime and making the Summer in Seaside Series come to life. She helped make this random thought I had one day, turn into an amazing multi-author collaboration. I would't have the Lancasters if we wouldn't have created this series!

Next I'd like to thank Sue Soares at SJS Editorial Services. You are amazing to work with. I appreciate your patience and flexibility. I simply love working with you. My books wouldn't be what they are without you.

To Jaime Ryter at The Ryter's Proof Editing Services, thanks for making my book pretty. Your proof reading put me at ease.

To the people who have supported me along the way, I'm

humbly grateful to have you in my life. Whether you've read my books, asked me about my progress, listened to me talk about my fictional characters as if they're a part of my family, plotted with me, or been my cheerleader, I appreciate your continued support. Please know it hasn't gone unnoticed.

Last but certainly not least, to my four beautiful girls who have turned into my task managers at times and who have had to wait patiently when I said, "Just one more minute," when I obviously meant a lot more than one.

I love that you get that I have deadlines and appreciate your not-so-subtle reminders that "Mom... you should be working" during my designated work time. I appreciate your support more than you'll ever know. I always look forward to celebrating with you and listening to our obligatory when my favorite two words of the book are written.

Even though you can't read this book—because that might be *weird*—for both of us, I love that you keep asking. I love you all more than words can express. You're the reason I continue to strive and reach for my goals each day.

# ABOUT THE AUTHOR

Amanda Shelley writes romantic stories you can escape into. Some are steamy, others are sweet but all have strong characters with a little bit of sass.

When not writing, Amanda enjoys time with her family, playing chauffeur, chef and being an enthusiastic fan for her children. Keeping up with them keeps her alert and grounded in reality. She enjoys long car rides, chai lattes and popping her SUV into four-wheel drive for adventures anywhere.

Amanda loves hearing from readers. Be sure to sign up for her newsletter and  follow her on social media. Join her reader's group Amanda's Army of Readers to stay up to date on her latest information.

Readers group:
https://www.facebook.com/groups/AmandasArmyofReaders/
Goodreads:
https://www.goodreads.com/author/show/19713563.Aman
da_Shelley
Newsletter:
https://geni.us/AmandaShelleyNL
www.amandashelley.com
Website:
www.amandashelley.com
Facebook:
https://www.facebook.com/authoramandashelley/

Instagram:

https://www.instagram.com/authoramandashelley/

Tik Tok:

https://www.tiktok.com/@authoramandashelley

Amazon:

https://www.amazon.com/author/amandashelley

Book Bub:

https://www.bookbub.com/profile/amanda-shelley

# ALSO BY AMANDA SHELLEY

*If you enjoyed this book, you will be happy to discover Amanda Shelley primarily writes in one world. For a complete list of the series reading order as well as a chronological time line, please visit:*

*https://amandashelley.com/reading-order/*

**The Summer Dare**

**Leave it to Nana to think of everything.**

After a grueling semester, I'm ready for a peaceful summer in Seaside with my sisters.

Imagine my surprise, when I'm woken by the screeching sound of a saw coming through my wall, the first official morning of break.

Not only did I come flying out of bed swinging, but I gave Ryan, the unsuspecting carpenter the surprise of his life, when I came wielding my killer coat hanger and all.

Too bad, I was only in a tank and undies and it wasn't nearly as effective as I'd hoped.

Of course, he insists he's only doing his job.

Since it's Nana's last request to care for us, I can't refuse.

However, I won't let a tall, pesky, sexy as sin, know-it-all get in my way of my summer plans. I pretend I ignore him - that is until my youngest sister pokes her nose in my business and throws down a dare I can't back down from.

Kiss the next single guy who walks up to the bonfire - or explain to my sisters why I get riled up over the contractor.

When Ryan suddenly appears, I know I'm screwed in more ways than one.

Not only will my sisters learn my secret, but from the determined look on Ryan's face, I'm afraid he's eager to reveal it to the world as well.

*What have I gotten myself into?*

As I walk toward him, one thing is certain - *this summer dare will either make or break me.*

https://geni.us/AmandaShelleyBooks

---

**The Summer Ultimatum**

**Watching my sister fall in love last summer gave me something I hadn't expected—hope**.

It gave me hope that there might be someone out there for me and hope that I might get past my misguided fears and finally let someone in.

With my help, Ryan's planning the most epic proposal. I just have to get the know-it-all musician I work with to fall in line to make it work.

Jax is wicked smart, extremely talented, and sexy as sin. But he can't see the forest for the trees when it comes to his potential. He'd rather keep playing in dive bars along the coast than take a real shot at success.

When the Seaside festival has a music competition, I present Jax with an ultimatum that will either make or break both our careers.

*I've laid it all on the line, but can he?*

https://geni.us/AmandaShelleyBooks

---

**The Summer Proposal**

**My sisters are dropping like flies.**

They're falling in love and having the time of their lives.

Don't get me wrong, I'm ecstatic for them. I love seeing them happy.

But I'm not ready for that type of commitment.

I can't even keep a plant alive, let alone find someone worthy of getting past a third date.

As the only sister done with school and single as a pringle, I have to do something fast, or I'll be my matchmaking aunt's next victim.

When Jax's drummer joins him for the summer and needs some help with his image, I make him a deal he can't refuse.

All is perfect—until I realize my summer proposal has one minor flaw.

***Our relationship may be a sham, but there's nothing fake about my feelings for Finn.***

https://geni.us/AmandaShelleyBooks

## The Summer Arrangement

**One, two, three—it's all down to me.**

As the youngest and only single Lancaster, I'm eager to spend my summer in Seaside, Oregon, with my sisters. It's something I've looked forward to all year, and I'm determined to make every minute count. After all, I've only got one year before I graduate from college and have to adult for real.

However, if I want to graduate debt free, I need to work. I have a lead on the perfect summer job with the nanny agency I've spent the last three summers catering to.

I just have to win over an adorable three-year-old and convince her single dad I'm the right one for the job.

Simple enough, right?

Except when I show up at his door, I'm shocked to find he's the guy I hooked up with last semester.

This cannot be happening.

I need this job. There's too much on the line to walk away.

*Maybe we can put the past behind us and make some sort of summer arrangement?*

---

**Zander: A Perfectly Independent Series Novella**

**(Available for free on All Retailers)**

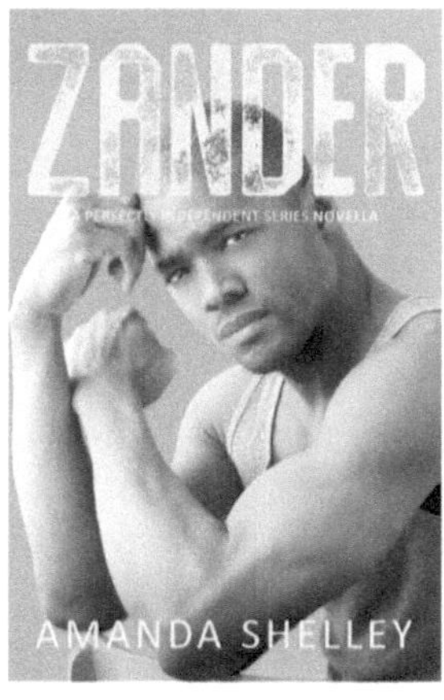

Zander's known for being a player both on and off the court. When his name shows up as my next client, my heart stalls, and not in a good way. There's no way I'll survive the semester with him. I just don't have the patience.

However, when I need help, Zander makes a proposal I can't refuse. He'll be my fake date to my best friend's wedding so I don't have to face my ex and his new girlfriend alone.

The weekend goes off without a hitch as we effortlessly pretend to have the time of our lives.

All is perfect... until I realize my feelings for Zander are no longer an act.

What will I do when our arrangement comes to an end?

https://geni.us/AmandaShelleyBooks

---

**Drew: Book One of the Perfectly Independent Series**

**Of all people, why him?**

He didn't EVEN bother to introduce himself, just assumed I knew him from his fame on the court.

Between his arrogance and the constant interruption from basketball groupies, there's no way I'll survive this semester. Sure, he's hotter than anyone I've ever laid eyes on in a science lab, but I can't afford to pull someone along to maintain the grade I deserve.

Just when I think my self-control is in check, he does something to remind me that he isn't the egotistical, self-centered jerk I thought he was.

With one stupid smile he makes my mind melt, my heart race, and my palms sweat.

*Will my perfectly laid out plans disappear, if I take a chance on Drew?*

https://geni.us/AmandaShelleyBooks

---

**Vince: Book Two of the Perfectly Independent Series**

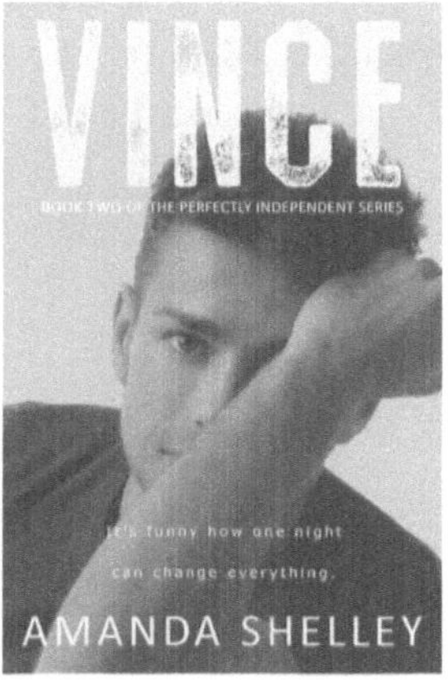


**It's funny how one night can change everything.**

As a bartender near campus, I'm certain I've heard it all. Rarely a shift passes without some guy taking his best shot, hoping I'll end my self-proclaimed dating diet.

Of course, this is exactly how I meet Vince.

Except, he isn't the one running his mouth.

No, he simply shuts down his idiotic friend, then stops my heart with the simplest of smiles and walks away.

Just when I force myself to forget him, he bumps into me on campus.

Our connection is consuming, and my world is knocked off kilter. It's far beyond physical attraction. He's smart, sexy, and feels like—*home?*

Wait, that can't be right...

Whatever it is, Vince has me breaking my rules to spend time with him.

My entire life I've prepared for meeting the wrong guys.

*What the hell should I do when I find the right one?*

https://geni.us/AmandaShelleyBooks

**Damien: Book Three of the Perfectly Independent Series**

Beautiful girls are not hard to find at Columbia River University.

The coeds on campus are great to look at but I was over that scene after graduation three years ago.

These days, outside of being part of the largest civil engineering job on campus, all I'm searching for is a decent meal and some peace and quiet. It's why I'm happy to have found what I consider a hidden gem in the diner I frequent.

All I need to do is finish this job and move on to the next by year's end.

Should be easy enough. Only when Vanessa walks up with a sexy smile and a mouth full of sass, she does more than take my order. She completely takes my breath away.

Next thing I know, I'm here every morning, making every excuse to dine with this intriguing woman. Not only is she smart and sexy, but she's laser focused on reaching the goals she's set for herself.

The more I get to know her, the more I'm convinced she's the one. I just have to find a way to get her to deviate from her perfectly laid plans and take a chance on me.

https://geni.us/AmandaShelleyBooks

**Making The Call**

Dani

As a bestselling romance author, most assume my life's glamorous, filled with combustible chemistry, and most of all, romance. Ha! I can only wish. With a deadline looming, I've escaped to my family's cabin on Anderson Island to free myself from distractions. My plan's great, until a man, who could pass as a cover model on one of my books, comes to my rescue. Is there chemistry? Sure. Is he everything I'd look for in a guy? Absolutely. But will my career be at risk if I give into my desire?

Luke

For a player, women line up outside the locker room. For coaches, we're lucky to get in the game. As the youngest NFL coach in the league, I live, eat, breathe, and even sleep football. To gear up for this season, I return to my home on Anderson Island for a much-needed break. When Dani literally crashes into my life, my mind's suddenly on the sexy brunette with a sailors mouth, rather than my team's next play. She has me dusting off another playbook entirely, making me wonder, did I make the right call?

https://geni.us/AmandaShelleyBooks

**The Boy Upstairs**

I ran into Derek while trying to escape the neighbor from hell.

Instantly, we hit it off. Since he's only here for three months and the microbrewery leaves me little time for commitments, it's the perfect setup for a fling.

He's adventurous, challenges me, and he just gets me from the inside out.

With our expiration date quickly approaching, I'm left to wonder... Will my heart ever be the same without the boy upstairs?

https://geni.us/AmandaShelleyBooks

**He Saved My Boy**

Davis is the first guy to catch my attention since... hell, I don't even know.

Instantly, he makes me think and feel things I've forgotten existed. It has been forever since I put my needs first, so I take the chance and let him light me up from the inside out.

Our night is the kind that will ruin me for all others.

But then I get the dreaded call.

I rush out without a second glance, knowing I'll likely never see him again.

My son will always come first—Always.

Imagine my surprise when Davis walks in, and I find he's the only one who can save my boy.

This cannot be happening—*I guess it's time to pull up my big girl panties and see what happens.*

https://geni.us/AmandaShelleyBooks

**The Vegas Pitch**

This pitch could make or break my career.

Not only will it set a personal record for the biggest account I've ever landed, but it could set my newfound company three years ahead of schedule for expansion.

Thank god I've got Nate Bellinger on my team.

Even though I had my reservations hiring the sexiest man I've ever laid eyes on – he more than meets my expectations with his hard work and determination. Together, we've formed a solid team and play off each other perfectly.

As we wait for the final verdict, I begrudgingly take Nate up on his offer for a night on the town. After all, this is Vegas and I need to let the chips fall where they may.

Imagine my surprise when I wake up the next morning to find we've not only won the campaign, but I'm apparently married to the man I've only ever let myself fantasize about.

The kicker of it all – he has no intentions of letting me go.

But what will it mean once we leave Vegas?

https://geni.us/AmandaShelleyBooks

# **Resilience:** Book One of Resilience Duet

# **Resolution:** Book Two of Resilience Duet

Samantha never saw Enzo coming.

As the dust settles from her divorce, her life is full. She doesn't have time for distractions. She's too busy running her own company and checking off numerous items from her kids' demanding schedule to have a life of her own.

Then he walks into her kitchen with his breathtaking green eyes and a mischievous grin. He's there to surprise his father - her contractor, but his presence makes everything off kilter.

Enzo's perfectly content with his adventurous life as an elite rescue pilot, until a harmless prank turns on him. Instead of surprising his father, he finds his world thrown off course by the beautiful woman with a sexy smile, wicked sass and the mouthwatering ability to keep him on his toes.

With his limited time on leave, is she worth the risk to his heart?

https://geni.us/AmandaShelleyBooks

## Collide: A Sweet Romance

Falling head over heels was the last thing I expected.

Literally.

Coffee is everywhere – and more than my ego is bruised.

When the handsome stranger I plowed into calls me by name, mortification sinks in.

He rushes off to class. I run home to change, hoping to forget the whole incident.

If only I could be so lucky.

I quickly find it's a small world and Gavin Wallace is completely unavoidable. Everywhere I turn he's there. In my classes. Hanging with my friends.

I've got his full attention and I have to admit, I like it a lot more than I should.

https://geni.us/AmandaShelleyBooks